A Big Problem

JOEY BETTANY SAT ON THE fence that railed in the garden of Die Rosen, her sister's chalet, whistling like a blackbird, and frowning profoundly. It was a bright, sunny day at the end of April, and a tiny fresh breeze tossed her uncovered black mop to a tangle that she would regret later. At present, she was so deep in thought about other things that she had no time to worry about her hair.

Tall and slim was Jo, with bright black eyes, set in a pointed face that was pale but healthy. In spite of her sixteen years, she looked more like fourteen, and her attitude on the fence – long, brown-stockinged legs coiled round the lower rail – bore this out. Once she had been delicate, but long years in the dry, health-giving atmosphere of the Tyrolean Alps had changed all that, and nothing proved it more surely than her position out there, with only a blazer over her deep-blue frock, worn as a sign that holidays were still in existence. A patter of small feet made her turn round, nearly overbalancing as she did so; and a sweet, high-pitched voice cried, "Oh, Joey – oh, Joey!"

Jo slipped down to the ground, and held out her arms to its owner. "Robinette! Where've you been, *Bübchen?*"

A little girl of nearly ten ran into the arms, and clasped her rapturously round the waist. Robin Humphries regarded Jo as her elder sister, and literally adored her. Jo returned the adoration with interest, and thought that she had never seen a dearer baby than "the Robin". For a moment, therefore, the two hugged each other; then Joey lifted the small girl up, swinging her to the fence, and put an arm round her to steady her. "Where have you been?" she repeated.

"I went to Gisela's to see Baby Natalie," replied the Robin, as she clutched Jo round the neck. "She wants you to go and see her tonight, Joey – but not me," she added.

"Well, you've just *been*," said Jo cheerfully. "Did she say why?"

"No; just that you were to go."

"Righto," said Jo.

The Robin gave her a little squeeze. "Tomorrow you go back to school, Joey dear," she said mournfully.

"But I'll be up for weekends," replied Jo consolingly. "You'll see more of me that way than you would even if you were going down with me."

The Robin's mouth drooped. "But I should see you each day – but *each* day," she said.

"My lamb, with me as head girl, that's about all you *would* see of me. As it is, I've a jolly good excuse for turning up rather oftener than I generally do at the Sonnalpe, and we'll be together all day long. And it isn't as if you'll be alone, either. There's David, and Baby Natalie. Peggy and Rix will be coming in another week. And you've got to keep an eye on Stacie, and help her to get through the time. You aren't awfully to be pitied, you know, Robin."

"And Tante Marguérite says I must stay, and so does Oncle Jem, so I must," added the Robin, with a little sigh.

"Quite true. Don't fret, darling. I'll be up as often as I can."

"Tante Marguérite says it's naughty to fret when things can't be helped," remarked the small girl, "but it's not easy, Joey."

"Don't I know it!" groaned Jo.

"What is the matter?" asked the Robin, with interest.

"Everything!" was the curt reply.

THE CHALET SCHOOL AND JO

Elinor M. Brent-Dyer

Collins
An imprint of HarperCollins*Publishers*

J91,863
£3·99

First published in Great Britain by W & R Chambers Ltd 1931
First published in paperback by Collins 1970
This impression 1998

1 3 5 7 9 10 8 6 4 2

Collins is an imprint of HarperCollins*Publishers* Ltd,
77–85 Fulham Palace Road, Hammersmith, London W6 8JB

ISBN 0 00 690344-4

Printed and bound in Great Britain by
Caledonian International Book Manufacturing Ltd, Glasgow, G64

The Robin nodded her head wisely. "*I* know. It is the being head girl that you don't like. But why, Joey? Me, I think it must be fun."

"Lot of fun, being responsible for everything," grumbled Jo. "No, Robin; you can't understand. But you will some day, I don't doubt."

"But you are head," persisted the Robin. "Everyone looks up to you, and you say how things are to be. I think that must be very nice."

Jo laughed half-heartedly. "And supposing I say things that go wrong? What about that, Robin?"

The Robin's lovely little face took on a look of gravity. "But you couldn't, Joey!"

"Couldn't I just! – There's the bell for *Kaffee*! Come on; I'll give you pickaback to the house. Cling tight!"

So saying, she took the Robin on her back, and galloped up the long path, through the awakening garden, and into the wide hall, where they were met by her elder sister, who frowned at the sight.

"Jo! How often have you been told not to do that? Robin is getting far too heavy for you."

She came forward, and lifted down the small girl as she spoke. Jo pulled a face. "It's the last day, Madge," she pleaded. "I shan't see her again for a bit. And I don't do it often since you and Jem made such a fuss about it."

Madge Russell shook her dark head, with its curly hair, and tried to look angry. "It's disobedience, Jo."

The Robin was there, so Jo refrained from the remark that she was getting rather too old to be kept in order now. She thought it, all the same, and her sister guessed it from her expression.

"Run along to the *Speisesaal*, Robin-a-Bobbin," she said to the child.

The Robin trotted off obediently, and the sisters faced one another in the hall.

"I'm not a baby now," said Jo.

Madge smiled. "No; that is true, Joey. But when it

comes to health, I'm afraid you must still be content to be treated as a child. You are so careless, Jo; and while you are growing at such a rate, it's necessary for you not to strain yourself in any way."

She laid one slim hand on Jo's shoulder, but that young lady shook it off ungraciously. "I must go and comb my hair. All right. I won't do it again; but I wish you and Jem didn't fuss so!"

She ran off down the hall to the stairs, and Madge stood looking after her with a sigh. Jo had been difficult these holidays. She resented the fact that she must grow up, and that this head girl post was a big step towards it. So far, Jo had managed to wriggle out of most responsibilities; but about this one, the Heads of the Chalet School had been firm. There was no one else so suitable, for of the elder girls in the school some were of much shorter standing, others were too quiet and too insignificant to be leaders.

The Chalet School, founded by Madge Russell nearly five years ago, and carried on, since her marriage with the brilliant young doctor who was head of the big sanatorium on the Sonnalpe, by a French friend who had been with her since the beginning, was a very dear treasure to her. The first five head girls had all done splendid work for it, and she was not minded to put an inferior one in the vacant place. Jo, with her strong character, vigorous personality, and great gift of charm, had been the obvious choice, and when she had been told about it, had first made an outcry, and then seemed to settle down to the idea. It was only these holidays that she had shown her sister how much she loathed the thought. She had been difficult and tiresome, resenting any attempts at control on the part of her sister, and showing an irritability quite foreign to her.

"I should like to give her a good shaking!" thought Madge, as she turned into the *Speisesaal*, where the rest of the family awaited her to take her place at the big coffee-urn.

"Where is Jo?" asked the doctor.

"Gone to tidy her hair," replied his wife, as she took her seat.

He laughed. "No wonder! I saw her on the fence a while ago, and she looked like a golliwog then."

Mrs Russell poured out the coffee, and the Robin carried round cups till Jo appeared, looking a little better for the severe brushing she had given her mop. Then the baby, as they all called her affectionately, though she was almost ten, ran up to her beloved, and demanded to know where she had been.

"Popped in to see Stacie," replied Jo, as she sat down on a pouffe.

Madge smiled, but said nothing. Stacie Benson was a member of the Chalet School who, owing to a rather serious accident the term before, had hurt her back, and was obliged to lie flat for the next few months. Seeing her was one of the ways in which Jo managed to reconcile herself to her fate. Even being head girl was not quite so bad as having to lie like that for months, as there seemed every prospect of Stacie having to do.

The meal went on quietly, only broken by Captain Humphries, the Robin's father, having to leave before the rest had finished, because an urgent phone message summoned him to the sanatorium, of which he was the general secretary. The Robin consumed her milk and sweet bread twists before she ran off to the nursery to play with Baby David for half an hour before his bedtime. Then Joey got up from her seat, and turned to her sister. "I'm going over to see Gisela, Madge. She told the Robin she wanted to see me."

"Very well," said Madge. "Put a coat on, though, Joey. The evenings are still cold, even if it *is* halfway through April."

Jo nodded, and went off to get into her big coat and school beret before she set off to the little chalet where Gisela Marani, the first head girl of the Chalet School, lived with her husband, Dr Gottfried Mensch, one of the assistants at the sanatorium.

The sun was setting over the great western mountains in a glory of crimson and saffron, which gilded the snow-capped peaks around the lake, lying far below. In the valley, twinkling lights showed that people there had already met the dusk which comes down quickly there. The lake itself lay dark beneath the sunset sky, its still waters mirroring the mountains in a lovely reflection which was discernible even as high up as the Sonnalpe.

Joey paused a moment to revel in the beauty before she turned down the path, and swung along to the Chalet das Pferd, so-called because a hunt was depicted in the frescos on the walls. At the door she stopped again to look at the glowing of the sky, then she went in quietly, shedding her beret and coat in the square hall, before she ran lightly up the stairs and tapped softly at a door on the upper landing.

"Come in, Joey," called a pleasant voice in German; and Jo opened the door and went into the big room, where Gisela lay on a couch, an old oak cradle at her side, in which reposed her newly-arrived daughter.

At sight of Joey the elder girl smiled, and held up a warning hand. "Come quietly, my Jo. Baby Natalie has just gone to sleep."

Jo tiptoed across the floor, and knelt down by the cradle that was more than two hundred years old, to peep at its newest occupant. "Isn't she a darling?" she murmured enraptured. "What enormous lashes she has! And she's going to be awfully like you, I think, Gisela."

Gisela laughed. "It's rather early to prophesy yet, Joey. Ring the bell, dear, and Nurse will come and move the cradle to the bedside. Then we can talk in comfort."

Joey did as she was bidden, and Nurse – a pleasant-faced Tyrolean from Innsbruck – came, and, with Jo's aid, lifted the cradle over to the bedside without rousing the little sleeper. Then, after a glance round to see that all was as it ought to be, she left the room again. "She's nice," said Jo appreciatively when she had gone.

"Very nice," said Gisela, flinging a cushion from the many against which she lay on to the floor beside her. "Come and sit down, Jo, and we'll have a good talk."

Jo subsided on the cushion, and turned her serious gaze on her friend.

"Well?" questioned Gisela.

"It seems so – well – *weird*, somehow, to think that you're a proud mamma, Gisela. It's only a year or two ago since you were head girl at school, and bossing us all round. Now you're married, and there's Baby Natalie."

"But it is very – happy," replied Gisela softly. "You will understand some day for yourself, Joey."

Joey shook her golliwog mop vigorously. "Not me! I'm not going to get married!"

"Nonsense!" replied Gisela calmly.

"Not nonsense at all!" protested Jo. "It's jolly good sense, I think! I'm going to have all the responsibility I care for – and *more*! – for the rest of my school life. I'm not taking on anything I haven't got to."

"That," said Gisela, with decision, "is cowardly."

"What?" Jo swung round on her.

"Well, do you not think so?"

"No, I don't. Gisela, what do you mean? *Why* is it cowardly to want to not grow up?"

Gisela laughed at the appalling lack of grammar, but she said gently enough, "The reason why you are so resenting this being head girl is because you are afraid of it."

"'Tisn't, then! It's because I don't want to have all my fun spoilt."

"It didn't spoil *my* fun – nor Juliet's nor Bette's – nor Grizel's."

"You're different, you crowd."

"I don't think Grizel is very different from you – in some ways."

11

Jo pondered this. "We've both done mad things in our time."

"Yes; and did Grizel go on doing mad things, once she was head?"

"No; and that's just what I mind about it. She got horribly grave and responsible. She wasn't like her old self at all. And that's what I mind. I wish Madge had never done it!"

Gisela sat up, and set her feet on the floor. "Don't you think you are being very selfish over it, Jo?"

Jo blushed. "I can't help it, Gisela. I was thrilled to hear I was to have another year of school; and then it was all spoilt by this."

"Not spoilt at all, Joey. Don't you want to feel that you have given the Chalet School something worth having in return for all that it has given you? And there's another thing to be considered. There is no other girl suitable for the post."

"Frieda – or Simone – or Marie," suggested Jo.

Gisela shook her head. "Frieda is too quiet. Simone is your shadow – and you know it. Marie is a dear, but she is no leader. No, Joey; you are the only one who could do it."

Jo shook herself impatiently. "You aren't much help!"

"Because I won't see things as you would like me to see them. Jo, how can I?" Gisela bent forward, and framed the sensitive troubled face in her hands. "It is no use fighting against it, Jo. It has to be. Why will you not accept it? You could make such a wonderful head girl if you chose."

"That's all you know about it," grumbled Jo.

"But it is true, Joey. You are a born leader. The girls all like you; they will follow you wherever you choose to lead them. It is rather a big thing, Joey dear, and I do so want you to rise to it."

"To hear you talk," said Jo, "anyone would think I was Queen Victoria being ordered to do things for the good of her country when she was a kid. A nation doesn't depend on it!"

"I'm not so sure," said Gisela thoughtfully. "A nation is largely what its women are. The wives and mothers and sisters have much to say in the moulding of the men. If we are not what we ought to be, how can we expect our men to be great?"

Joey was silent.

"Madame is such a wonderful mother with David," went on Gisela. "I mean to model myself on her. He is so well trained already, though he is only a baby."

"Gisela!" Jo suddenly interrupted her. "I've got an idea!"

Gisela waited for it, though she wondered what was coming next. Some of Jo's ideas were wild in the extreme. As for Jo, thankful to have side-tracked the conversation, she plunged into it at once. "Look here! David will be just the right age. They'll be practically brought up together. What's the matter with seeing that he and Natalie marry each other when they are grown up?"

Whatever else she had expected, it is safe to say that Gisela had not expected this, and after staring at her friend for a moment in speechless silence, she lay back among her cushions, and laughed till she nearly cried.

"I don't see where the funny side comes in," said Jo, when Gisela had finally recovered herself. "As a matter of fact, it's all carrying on that idea of yours that a nation is what we choose to make it. The babies will have the advantage of the marvellous training you and Madge are going to give them. Well, then, *their* children ought to be wonders at the very least!"

Gisela sat up again, and mopped her eyes. "Don't try to be sarcastic, Jo. We shall do our best, but we've got to take into account what they are themselves. But – to matchmake for two babies like that—" Words failed her.

Jo got to her feet. "Now don't you go off again," she

warned, "or I'll fetch Nurse. You'll be having hysterics if you're not careful."

The door opened, and Dr Gottfried Mensch came in. He was a tall young man, with a mane of yellow hair, and kindly blue eyes. He looked started as he heard the sound of his wife's laughter, and heard Joey's diatribe.

"*Gut' Abend*, Joey. – But why are you laughing so, *Weibling*?" he asked.

"It's just because I said Natalie and David ought to get married when they grow up," said Joey in aggrieved tones. "Then Gisela went off like this, and giggled like an idiot!"

Gottfried Mensch chuckled. "It is not very surprising. I wonder what you will suggest next?"

"That it's time I was going." Jo stretched herself. "Heigh-ho! I shan't see you for a week or two now, my dear. Natalie will have grown quite a lot when next I call."

"How soon are you coming up, Joey?" asked Gisela, her fit of laughter over.

"Well, not for two or three weeks at any rate. I'm not very sure. Madge said I should come oftener this term, as the Robin will be here; but you know what the first weeks of term are like."

"I know." Gisela stretched out a hand and pulled Joey down to her. "And you go so early tomorrow, my Jo, I shall probably be asleep."

"Seven o'clock," nodded Jo. Then with a little, shamefaced squeeze of the slender hand in hers, she added, "And – and – I'll think it over – what you've said. Anyhow, I'll have to do the best I can, because, after all, if you're head, you're head."

She kissed Gisela goodbye after that; stole over for a final peep at Baby Natalie; and then ran off to spend what was left of the evening with her sister, the Robin, and – for ten minutes – with Stacie.

Left to themselves, the Mensches exchanged glances.

"Jo hates it now, but it will be good for her," said Gisela.

"The best thing in the world. She should grow up, at nearly seventeen. She has remained a child too long," said Gottfried. "Madame is very wise."

"She always is," replied his young wife. "There! I hear Baby awakening. Give her to me, *Herzliebst*."

Gottfried lifted his tiny daughter out of the old cradle, and brought her to her mother. Gisela took her very tenderly, and held the mite closely to her. "All this must come to her, too," she said presently.

"That is life," he said philosophically.

"I wonder what Jo will give the school during this last year?" said Gisela.

"That is a big question," he replied. "But to me, an even bigger one is what will the school give to Jo?"

"Ah, that we shall see when the time is ended," said his wife, as she rocked the baby in her arms to sleep again.

CHAPTER II

The Term Begins

"AND THERE'S THE SCHOOL AT last! Thank goodness! I'm sick and tired of travelling!"

The one or two early visitors to the Tiernsee looked with a smile at the bright-faced schoolgirl who had spoken. They were English, so the clear words meant something to them. They had been rather surprised at the crowd of girls, all in long brown coats and berets to match, who had scrambled into the Innsbruck–Kufstein train at Innsbruck, and left it with themselves at Spärtz, the little town at the foot of the mountains up which they must go to reach the Tiern valley. When they had found there another group of schoolgirls waiting for these, they had opened their eyes, for they had no idea that there was a school anywhere near. When the throng of girls had formed up into orderly lines with the little ones between the bigger ones, and had set out up the mountain path, they had been more surprised still. They themselves had gone up by the way which lay at the other side of the railway that ran between the Tiernsee and Spärtz in the season, and had just met with the girls again. They turned involuntarily and looked in the direction in which the speaker had waved. They saw a big chalet (which they might have mistaken for a hotel if they had not overheard her), surrounded by a high fence, while a little way from it, and also embraced by the circling fence, was a smaller house.

"A school!" said the younger one of the two ladies who stood with the tall man, resting for a moment. "What a gorgeous place to have it!"

"Bonny set of girls too," he said. "Hello! Is this a young whirlwind coming along?"

It was only Joey Bettany, however, tearing along to greet her chums. She had reached Briesau, the village on the banks of the Tiernsee where the school was situated, by half-past nine that morning, to find that she was the first, and none of the others would be there till the afternoon. It was a pity, but it could not be helped. The doctors at the Sonnalpe had to get back, so the early start had to be made. Some of the staff were there already, of course. Miss Annersley, the senior mistress, had been thankful to see the new head girl, and had pressed her into service, as soon as the milk and rolls provided for a second breakfast – the first had been eaten at six – had been disposed of. All the morning Jo had been busy with the piles of new stationery, helping to unpack them and

16

stow them away in the enormous cupboard that stood in the wide passage leading to the big form rooms. They had finished just before the bell rang to summon them to *Mittagessen*, and then Miss Annersley, busy with time-tables, had sent the head girl off for a walk.

"The others won't be here till four o'clock," she had said. "It's a lovely day, and a shame to waste it indoors if there's no need. Off you go, and have a stroll. What about a walk along to Geisalm to see what the Dripping Rock is doing?"

Joey agreed, and set out, but she was a gregarious young person as a rule, and she felt very dull on her lonely walk. Indeed, she only went as far as the Dripping Rock – so called because a tiny stream from the alm above fell by way of a jutting-out of the cliff into the lake – and then returned, to wander round the school and wish the others would come.

At half-past three she had gone to the study to ask permission to walk along to Seespitz, the tiny hamlet at the end of the lake to meet the others, and had been given it. Then she had been sent to make herself tidy first, in case any strangers should be there, and, hearing the voices carrying on the still air while she was still some distance away from the *Gasthaus* where the mountain path came out into the valley, had had to run to be there in time. Hence, her wild descent on them.

She was at once surrounded by a shrieking, welcoming crowd, who thronged round her, demanding to know if she had had good holidays – how Stacie was – if David had any more teeth – what Baby Natalie was like, and if Gisela was well. Finally, she refused to speak till they were all quiet, and Miss Stewart, one of the mistresses in charge, called for silence. "Now, Jo?" she said, smiling.

Jo looked round at them with dancing eyes. "Everyone is splendid," she said. "David has three new teeth, and is getting *huge*. Madame sent her love and best wishes for the new term to everybody. Stacie is going on all right, and they hope to be able to raise her a very little in another week's time. It's going to be a fairly long job, they're afraid, but they say she ought to be able to get about in an invalid chair by September, and then she'll come back into school. She's very fit otherwise, and sent her love to everyone – 'specially you, Margia. My sister wants you and one or two of the others to go up on Saturday after Guides to spend the weekend. Some of us are going every weekend to make things amusing for Stacie and the Robin—"

"How is Robin, Joey?" asked Miss Stewart anxiously.

"Much stronger; almost herself again," replied Jo. "She's not to come back this term, though."

"Oh, why not?" protested a small, fair girl, Amy Stevens by name.

"The doctors think she'll be better up there when the summer heats come," explained Jo. "It's all right, Amy. You are going up with Margia and Evvy, and one or two of the others on Saturday, so you'll see her soon."

Miss Wilson, the science mistress, nodded. "Good! Well, as we seem to be blocking the way, I think we had better move on now. The rest of the news can wait till we get back to the Chalet. Form lines, girls. – Cornelia, why are you leaving your case behind? Don't you want it?"

"I forgot it," acknowledged Cornelia, a fair girl of fourteen, with enormous blue eyes, and a chin that Joey had once characterised as "first cousin to a ramrod".

"Pick it up, and don't be silly. – Now; are we all ready? Then – forward!"

The girls set out on the last stage of their journey, and the visitors, now that they had gone, turned to their own guide, and asked him which way they had to go. On learning they were for the *Gasthaus* at Buchau, another little hamlet at the other side of the lake, he indicated the way, adding, "That was the Chalet School, gracious ladies. The school of St Scholastika is at Buchau, but their young ladies do not return till the morrow."

"*Two* schools up here!" exclaimed the younger lady.

"But yes, *gnädiges Fräulein*. The air is good here, and they say it is excellent for the young ladies."

Having said this, he dropped the subject, and led the way across the water meadows towards the hamlet.

Meanwhile, the Chalet School – or as much of it as had come, went on its way chattering gaily in not one, but seven different languages. Girls of all nationalities were pupils here. Some had parents up at the Sonnalpe for treatment, who, having heard of the school, had had their girls sent out to it, so that they might be near. Others had been told of the excellent education and training the girls received, and had applied for the first vacancy. Already the school, opened but five years before, numbered more than eighty girls, and workmen had come up the week before, and were very busy erecting another chalet to be the exclusive property of the Middles when it should be done. Not many of the elder girls would be leaving at the end of this year, and applications had been numerous for the coming one. Therefore, Mrs Russell and Mademoiselle Lepâttre, the two Heads, had decided to build. This information Joey imparted to her own special friends as they went along.

"My sister told me that if they accepted all the new girls they have been offered for next term, there would be more than a hundred in the school," she said, as she walked between Frieda Mensch, a pretty girl of the fair North German type, sister to Dr Gottfried Mensch, and Simone Lecoutier, a little French girl, whose quick-glancing black eyes in a little sallow face, and neatly cropped black head, were as great a contrast to Frieda's apple-blossom colouring, long fair plaits, and blue eyes, as could be imagined.

"More than a hundred, Joey?" cried Frieda. "But that is splendid!"

"Isn't it?" agreed Jo enthusiastically. "So they are

building another chalet, and what we shall call it goodness only knows. We've got *The* Chalet, and Le Petit Chalet already. Madame says we must think up something for her."

"Have we any *nouvelles* this term?" asked Simone.

"Only three – which is rather lucky, for where we'd have put any more is beyond me," said Jo.

"Oh? Where are they to be?" asked Frieda.

"One Junior, and two Middles," answered Jo. "The junior is German, and the Middles are English – two girls from Taverton – *you* know; the place where we lived before we came here. I don't know them – they must have gone there since we left. Their names are Faith and Mercy Barbour, so goodness knows what they are like! They aren't coming till Saturday, because there was some difficulty about the escort."

By this time they had reached the gate in the high fence that cut off the school from the curiosity of the visitors that throng to the Tiernsee in the summer months, and were streaming in, so the conversation ceased, for Mademoiselle was on the doorstep to welcome them back, and Jo had to stop talking.

It was easy to see that the girls loved their school. Their bright faces as they answered the Head's greetings, and the alert way in which, those over, they darted off to their various dormitories to disrobe were all proof of that. Frieda, Joey, and Simone, with a quiet Austrian girl, Carla von Flügen, and a pretty Italian, Bianca di Ferrara, were in what was known as the Green dormitory, which was at the top of the house, having big windows looking out on the Tiernsee at one end, and equally big ones from which you could see right up the valley towards the great Tiern Pass at the other.

Joey as head girl, and Frieda as second prefect, had first choice of cubicles, and they took the two Tiern windows. The others settled themselves in happy-go-lucky fashion, Carla, as the youngest, having the "door" cubicle. Then they unpacked their hand-cases, picked up their berets and coats, and ran downstairs to the Senior cloakroom, where they found some of the other Seniors already "bagging" pegs and lockers. That duty ended, they retired to the big common room they shared with the senior Middles, and then tongues ran fast and fluently.

Joey, trilingual as the result of her years in the Tyrol, and with more than a smattering of Italian, carried on four conversations at once. Term had not yet begun as far as rules were concerned, and they were able to use their native tongues for today.

"We must have a prefects' meeting tomorrow," said Jo presently.

"There's a good deal to be decided, isn't there?" asked Carla.

"A good deal," agreed Jo. "For one thing, we've got to fix on a new librarian—"

"Joey! But why?" demanded Frieda.

"Because if I'm head girl, that's one person's job," replied Jo. "I can't carry on with the library as well."

"No-o; I suppose not," acknowledged Frieda. "There is a great deal of work attached to the library, I know. But whom shall we choose?"

"That we must decide at the meeting," said Jo, as pretty Luise brought in the coffee, and she got up to go and pour it out.

"What about the magazine?" asked Simone, as she followed to help.

"I wish I knew!"

"There is no one else to do it as well as you, my Jo. I think you must remain editor."

"Nonsense!" said Joey irritably. "Come to that, what about yourself? You subbed for me when I was ill last autumn."

Simone turned a horrified face on her. "*Jamais!*" she cried. "*Mais jamais!*"

"All right; *jamais* if you like. We'll see what we decide

J 91, 863

at the meeting," replied Jo. "Meanwhile, if you're so extravagant with the sugar, we'll all be rationed before we know where we are."

Simone looked down at the cup, into which she had put four pieces of sugar, and blushed. "I did not notice," she confessed.

The others came thronging round them now, demanding the coffee, and some of the Middles passed baskets filled with twists of sweet bread and little crisp cakes, all honey and nuts. *Kaffee und Kuchen*, as this meal is called, was always an informal affair, never attended by any of the staff. The prefects kept order, and poured out, and the girls thoroughly enjoyed this one meal they might have alone.

"Does Mademoiselle speak with us after *Kaffee*?" asked Bianca, when all had been served, and they were sitting about the room in groups.

"Yes; but she doesn't want us for long," replied Jo. "There aren't any new staff this term, and we pretty much know what's coming in the way of work, and so on. The Hobbies Club will be shelved, of course – unless it's a very wet summer," she added.

"Madame's birthday is this term," said Simone. "What shall we do for it, Jo?"

Jo shook her head. "I haven't the least idea. Probably we shan't know till nearer the time."

But there she was mistaken. When, *Kaffee* ended, they had cleared the remains away, and were sitting, ready for Mademoiselle Lepâttre's short welcoming speech, they all got a shock of the most pleasant kind; for after greeting them, and wishing them all a happy term, she said with a smile, "And now, *mes chères*, I have some pleasing news for you. This year we celebrate our dear Madame's birthday at the half term, instead of on the day. We – all here present – shall go to Oberammergau on the Monday, and stay there till the Saturday, that we may see the great Passion Play."

She made a few other remarks, but she might as well have talked Greek to them for all they took in of her further words. The news that they were to be taken to see the Passion Play, of which all had heard so much, filled their minds to the exclusion of everything else, and Jo only voiced the feelings of everyone when she cried after the staff had taken their departure, "The Passion Play! One of the dreams of my life fulfilled! Madge is a *dream* to have thought of such a topping way of celebrating her birthday!"

CHAPTER III

The Prefects' Meeting

THE PREFECTS' MEETING TOOK PLACE at eight o'clock that evening. By that time the Sixth form had all finished their unpacking, and while Matron attended to the rest, the grandees of the school met in solemn conclave, in the pretty little room that had been given them when the school first began.

Jo, taking the chair at the head of the table, as was her right, felt unaccountably shy, and wished herself miles away. She had never felt that about sitting in one at the side of the table. She had generally enjoyed the meeting before. Now she felt as if the eyes of all were upon her – as they were not, since Simone Lecoutier and Eva von Heiling were disputing over a chair which both wanted.

The noise they made finally woke Joey from her trance, and she turned on the combatants with a sharp,

23

"That'll do! Simone! Come up here beside me."

Simone walked demurely round the table, and took her seat beside the head girl. Eva, a fair-haired young person of nearly seventeen, sat down on the disputed chair, and they were ready.

"What's the first business?" asked Jo calmly.

"Last term's report," replied Frieda. "I have it here, Joey. Shall I read it?"

Jo nodded, and Frieda read out the report in her soft, pretty voice.

"Yes; I think it's all there," said Jo, when it was ended. "Any objections to anything in it? No? Very well, then; I'll sign it." She signed it in her untidy script, and pushed the book back to Frieda. "Duties next, I suppose," she said, as the second prefect carefully blotted the signature, and closed the book. "This will take some settling this year. For one thing, I can't continue as librarian. I shall have quite enough to do otherwise."

"But, Joey!" cried Bianca di Ferrara.

"I shall. It's no use trying to keep it on, Bianca. I couldn't do it property. There's a good deal of work attached, one way and another. I don't want to give it up, because I've always loved doing it. However, it can't be helped. So will you think it over for a minute."

"I propose Sophie Hamel for it," said Frieda, rising in her place. "She reads a great deal, and she has done it on occasions when Jo has been absent. She is one of our oldest girls, and would do it well, I think."

"Good scheme," agreed Jo, forgetful of the fact that her position debarred her from making suggestions. "I think Sophie would be – er – very good as librarian."

"I will second the proposal," said Carla von Flügen, who knew exactly what *her* duty would be – that of music monitress. She learned the piano with the visiting master, Herr Anserl, and knew his ways. He was an irritable creature, and the post was not one desired by anyone, as Carla knew. The only other member of the prefects to learn with him, Vanna di Ricci, lived in mortal dread of him, and would certainly have driven him wild with her meticulous neatness and order.

Jo sat back in her chair. "Going – going – I mean, hands up everyone who wants Sophie for librarian," she said.

Eight hands waved wildly in the air, including her own, and the matter was settled.

"Hobbies Club we don't have to bother about this term," said Jo, when order was regained once more, and Frieda had duly noted down the appointment in her minutes. "Carla, you'll take on Music, won't you? You know Herr Anserl; and you can give an eye to Cicero," she added, referring to their eccentric singing master.

Carla nodded. "Very well, Jo. I suppose I must," she said dismally.

Jo grinned at her. "Poor old thing! Never mind; he doesn't rage at you as he used to at Grizel," she said. "The only other person is Vanna, and—"

"Not for worlds!" exclaimed Vanna, with a gesture of horror.

"I quite agree," murmured Marie von Eschenau. "If Vanna were Music, none of his pupils would live to tell the tale!"

Vanna laughed. "I am sorry it leaves it to Carla," she said. "But he is so untidy, and I should always be making things neat, and then—"

"Then, my love, he would curse you," said Jo calmly. "*That's* fixed, then. What next?"

"Games captain," suggested Simone.

"Marie will do that, of course. – You will, won't you, Marie?"

Marie nodded. "Yes; thank you."

"Stationery? – Frieda, do you feel equal to coping with the stationery and the Juniors?"

"Of course," said Frieda, with a smile.

"Good! Then Frieda takes on Stationery, and Simone

25

will do form rooms and the staff room. It only means seeing that the various monitresses don't slack off their duties. *You* don't have to pick up after people."

Simone nodded. "Yes, my Jo. And what about Break duty?"

"I will, if I may," said Vanna. "Indeed, Jo, it is only fair, for the rest of you have plenty to do, and it is nothing but to see that the girls get their milk and biscuits, and that the staff coffee is taken to the staff room at break."

Jo looked dubious. "It'll mean all your breaks being booked," she objected. "Yes; I know Lisa did it last year; but then, she *was* a day-girl, and got no prep or early morning duties. You are a boarder, and will get them like the others."

"Still, I do not mind," said Vanna. "I should like to do it, Joey."

"Oh, all right," said Jo. "Vanna, then, for Break duty, Frieda. – And Bianca, will you do Junior duty? It only means prep, and they finish in an hour, so it won't take you too much off your own work. – Eva will see to the Pets section. As she knows most of what there is to know about animals, she's the best choice for it."

Eva laughed. "I don't know a great deal," she said. "I'll do my best, Joey."

"And saints couldn't do more," agreed Jo. "As for me, well – I'm head girl, which is one person's work at any time. Also, for this term at any rate, I'm going to keep on the editorship of *The Chaletian*. I can't do it in the winter – I'll have twice as much to see to then. But I can manage in the summer, I think; and I'm going to train on my new editor so that she can begin fair with the new school year."

"Who is she to be, Joey?" asked Simone.

The rest looked at the head girl eagerly. They were as curious as Simone on this point.

"Stacie Benson," said Jo calmly.

There was a petrified silence on the part of all. Frieda

finally broke it. "But, Jo, she is a very new girl – and she won't be here this term," she added.

"That doesn't matter," said Jo airily. "I shall be up there quite a lot, and I want contributions in early, so that she can have them." She leant forward in her chair, her eyes glowing with eagerness. "Listen, all of you! I know poor Stacie left an unpleasant impression last term; but she's not a bit like that now. It'll keep her occupied while she's got to be up at the Sonnalpe. Also she knows a good deal, and has read more than most of us. She'll give us her very best, I know. Won't you agree?"

"I will," said Simone, who had never yet been known to decide against her beloved Jo.

Jo nodded at her, but looked at the rest anxiously. She was very keen on this appointment, but she knew that it might be difficult to secure it. Stacie, or, to give her her full name, Eustacia Benson, had been a difficult girl. Brought up by a professor father and a doctor mother, both middle-aged, and both full of theories which they had practised on their unfortunate child, she had come to school with a preconceived hatred for all schools and all girls. A stormy term had ensued, and though things had ended better than might have been expected, Jo knew that many of the girls still disliked the English child who was now up at the Sonnalpe, condemned to lying on her back till September at least, owing to her own silliness. But this accident had made a great change in the girl who had been so cordially disliked. There was good stuff in her, though it had been overlaid with a thick veneer of priggishness, and the long weeks of suffering had peeled off this till Eustacia had vanished, to leave behind her Stacie, an infinitely more likeable person.

It was in the hopes that the editorship would give her something to do, and help to bind her firmly to the school that she had once most cordially disliked, that Jo had pressed forward her claims.

But Jo was the only one to see this. Simone followed Jo, and Frieda could generally be trusted to grasp at what lay behind such an action. Still, even so supported, Jo knew quite well that she could not carry out her plan unless some of the others would join with them. The question was – would they?

Marie von Eschenau was the first to speak. A strikingly lovely girl, good at games, and with a charm of manner that only came second to Jo's, she had a considerable following in the school, and the head girl listened to what she had to say with deep anxiety. "I do not quite understand," she said. "Is it that you will take up to Eus – Stacie – all the contributions, and permit her to make selections from them for *The Chaletian*?"

"That's more or less the idea," acknowledged Jo. "Of course, I shall be final judge; but Stacie shall have a fair chance to show what she's made of. Won't you agree to it, you people?"

"But why Stacie?" asked Eva at length.

"Because she's got brains when she cares to use 'em," returned Jo. "She can write when she likes. She's fearfully methodical – worse than Vanna, if that's possible. She would be just, I think. Last of all, she made a rotten beginning, and she's got a nice punishment for it all! I want to give her a hand if I can, and I think this would be quite a decent way of doing it. You needn't worry about the mag's being let down – *I'll* see to that! Girls! Won't you back me up?"

Sophie nodded. "Yes, Jo. I will, for one."

"So will I," said Frieda. She turned to the others. "We all will. Jo is right about it. After all, she'll still be there, and if Stacie is of no use as editor, then we must just choose someone else next term."

Those words turned the scale. The rest agreed to let Stacie have her chance, and Jo, with a warm feeling round her heart, dismissed the meeting after one or two minor matters had been discussed. As they walked downstairs to the common room, the head girl slipped her hand through Frieda's arm. "*Brick* you are!" she murmured.

Frieda smiled. "The first brick was you, Joey," she said. "It is your doing mainly, you know. I was glad to back you up."

Then they reached the room, and unsentimental Jo, with a horror of being caught, pulled away her hand, and marched off to ask Margia Stevens, leader of the Middles, where the new girls were.

CHAPTER IV

A Little Prep

"Heigh-ho! Prep again! I don't know where a thing is!"

"That's your own fault! What have you lost *now*, Margia, my lamb?"

Margia Stevens turned a frowning face on her friend, Elsie Carr, a pretty, dark girl of fourteen, and said, "I like you saying it's my own fault! You know quite well that Charlie has gone and moved all the lockers round, and nobody ever knows where anything is these days."

"Well, it's not much use saying that to Charlie," returned Elsie calmly. "You know what nuts she is on keeping things tidy. Tell me what it is you've lost, and I'll help you to find it – or them."

Margia crossed over to the long row of lockers where the girls kept their books, and knelt down by one which, when she opened the door, promptly sent an avalanche of books, papers, and other débris on to her. Elsie joined her.

"Well, for one week, I must say I think you've got going fairly well," remarked the latter.

Margia began picking up the papers, while her chum collected the exercise books, and piled them up neatly.

"I want my geog book," said the malcontent presently.

"Here you are!" Elsie pulled it out from the bottom of the pile, and offered it with a flourish. "What else?"

Margia glanced at the timetable pinned to the inside of the door. "Geom – filthy stuff—"

"Slang, Margia? Pay the usual fine, please," said a cold voice behind them.

The two turned round, to see Miss Wilson regarding them with an unpleasant air.

"Why are you here now?" asked the mistress. "Preparation began ten minutes ago, and you ought to be there now."

"We were practising, Miss Wilson," said Elsie, getting to her feet.

"When does your practice-time end?"

"At half-past five," replied Elsie reluctantly.

"And do you wish me to understand that you have taken all this time to put away your music, collect your books – which should have been ready for you – and *yet* you are here talking?"

No answer from the two culprits, who stood looking uncomfortable.

"I am waiting for an answer, girls," she reminded them sharply when the silence had become oppressive.

"No-o-o, Miss Wilson," said Margia slowly.

"Then what have you been doing?"

"Nothing – much," said Elsie.

"What is it?"

"Only talking, Miss Wilson."

"Indeed?" The mistress glanced down at her watch.

"Well, you have now wasted fifteen minutes of your preparation, so I am afraid you must make it up after supper. Finish getting your books, Margia; and Elsie, go at once. Margia can find her things for herself." She paused, and looked at the chaos on the floor. "When you have finished your prep," she said, "I think you had better tidy your locker. Take an order mark, both of you, for being here talking out of hours. – And Margia, take another for the disgraceful condition of your locker. You ought to be ashamed of yourself."

With this, she walked off to the table, picked up the magazine which had brought her to the common room, and left them. Elsie gathered up her own books, and went slowly to the door.

"Get on," said Margia. "You know what Bill is! Sorry *you* got into the row as well."

Knowing what "Bill" was, Elsie vanished; and Margia, feeling thoroughly at odds with the world, finished collecting her possessions, rammed such of them as she did not need back into the locker, slammed the door on them, and followed Elsie into the big form room where Joey Bettany was taking prep.

The head girl looked up as this latest comer trailed in with a great clatter of dropped books. "A little more quietly, please, Margia," she said.

"Sorry," mumbled Margia, dropping her pencil-box with an additional clatter.

Doubtful whether it was an accident or not, Jo contented herself with a frown, and turned back once more to her loathed algebra. Margia picked up the box, dumped everything down on her desk, and sat down at it. After glaring at the untidy heap before her for a moment, she selected her geography book and atlas, and put the rest on the floor at her feet. Then she settled herself to making a barely recognisable outline of the map of Australia. Drawing was not one of Margia's strong points.

By the time the map was finished there was very little

surface left on the paper, but a good many rubber crumbs were there. Then she discovered that she had left her mapping-pen in her locker. Leaning forward, she dug Anne Seymour of her own form in the back. Anne, in the middle of ruling a neat line under a carefully-worked geometry problem, started, dug her pen into the page with a wild splutter, and exclaimed aloud.

Jo raised her eyes. "What is the matter, Anne?" she demanded.

"I – er—" began Anne feebly, while she hunted madly in her mind for an excuse that Jo would be likely to accept.

Margia stood up. "It was my fault, Joey. I dug her."

"Why?" demanded Joey crossly. She had been getting into appalling difficulties over a difficult sum in algebraic progression, and was not too well pleased at being interrupted.

"I wanted to borrow her mapping-pen."

"Where's your own?"

"In my locker – I *think*."

"Don't you *know*?"

"Er – I'm not very sure."

"In other words, your locker is so untidy that it's hard for you to say what you have or haven't got in it, I suppose," said Jo, who was not herself famed for being tidy.

Margia coloured furiously, and looked down. Jo proceeded to enlarge on it. "I wish you Middles would try to keep your things in their proper places," she said – and the injustice of such a remark from Joey Bettany, who had had a name for never knowing where anything she owned was at a given moment, roused all Margia's worst temper – "you never have a thing when you ought. You can go and look for your pen. I'll time you, and you can come after *Abendessen* and make up what you lose now."

"Oh – *hang*!" muttered the culprit, who had planned to spend her free time that evening in a very different way, and was moved out of all caution at this.

Unfortunately for her, Joey heard her. "I beg your pardon?" she said icily.

Margia shuffled her feet, and made no reply.

"That was slang, wasn't it?"

"I suppose so."

"Then you can pay a fine – and take an order mark for being rude into the bargain."

Margia marched off, slamming the door behind her. Luckily, Jo had enough tact not to call her to account for it. She had seen that the other girl was in a furious temper, and judged it best to let the thing slide. Besides, Margia had been one of her chums when *she* was a Middle, and she rather disliked having to pull her up. Margia hunted for her pen for a good three minutes before she found it, and by the time she had returned to the prep room, she had another seven to add to the fifteen Miss Wilson had already imposed on her. She sat down in sulky silence, and began to ink in her map. Jo heaved a sigh, and buried herself once more in her algebra.

However, there was to be little peace for the head girl this evening. She had just discovered a careless mistake which obliged her to rework the whole of one sum, when a double crash and a wild shriek roused her from her own task in time to see Cornelia Flower and Ilonka Barkocz, a quiet Hungarian girl, rising from the floor, where their two desks lay in a muddle, with the ink from both meandering over the polished boards. With the fear of "Matey" before her eyes, Jo sent Cornelia flying for cloths and water, and put Ilonka to setting up the desks again. When the ink had been mopped up and order restored, she demanded an explanation of the incident.

"I – upset," returned Cornelia lamely.

"What on earth were you doing to get upset?"

Cornelia remained discreetly silent. As a matter of fact, she had been tilting her chair backwards, had tilted too far, clutched at Ilonka's desk, and involved her next-door neighbour in the catastrophe. Tilting was strictly forbidden, since Amy Stevens had stunned herself once as the result of overdoing it, and Cornelia was a bad offender this way. She knew that she would get short shrift from the head girl if she gave the true explanation, so she sought refuge in silence.

"I suppose you mean you were tilting?" said Joey at length.

Cornelia judged silence to be the best thing, so she said nothing.

"Take your learning work and stand for the rest of prep," said the exasperated Jo.

"There's only rep left, and I've arithmetic and French to write!" protested Cornelia.

"Then you can come back after *Abendessen*, and do them before you go to bed. For once, you can know your rep – there's a good three-quarters of an hour left of prep," said Jo inflexibly.

Cornelia grimaced at this edict, but said nothing more. The head girl turned her attention to Ilonka. "What were *you* doing?" she demanded.

"It was my fault," said Cornelia. "Lonny was doing nothing – I fell against her."

"I see. Pick up your things, Ilonka, and get on, *do*!"

Ilonka did as she was told, and prep went on in silence for a short while. But the Middles seemed to be possessed tonight, and before long there was another disturbance. Evadne Lannis and Violet Allison, a quiet girl of thirteen, were sharing a history book, Evadne's having met with an accident two days previously. The new ones had not yet arrived, so Miss Stewart had ordered the small American to borrow from someone else. Seeing that Jo was busily occupied with her algebra, which was still proving troublesome, Evadne had pulled her chair closer to Violet's desk, and was looking over with her, though this was strictly forbidden. Violet, reading more slowly than her chum – or paying more attention to what she read – had not quite finished when Evadne turned the page. Violet pushed her hand out of the way, bent on reading the last paragraph. The hand caught the top of the inkwell and away it went, all over the floor, bespattering Cyrilla Maurús liberally on its way. Cyrilla uttered an exclamation which was echoed by Violet and Evadne, and Jo, with a weary sigh, gave up the struggle with her own work, and descended from her perch to demand what was happening *now*.

"I made Evadne upset her ink, please, Joey," said Violet, who stood in considerable awe of the head girl.

"What on earth were you doing to do that?" demanded Jo crossly. "You kids all seem to be off your heads tonight. Go and get the things and mop up, Violet. – And what's your chair doing over here, anyhow, Evadne?"

"I – was sharing Violet's history," faltered Evadne.

"Then you can just take an order mark. You know jolly well it isn't allowed. I'm ashamed of you!" With which Jo, having seen Violet clear up the mess, and sent Cyrilla to change her frock, stalked back to the desk once more, in no very good humour.

Ten minutes later, a crash of books roused her from her literature, which she had taken up, despairing of ever doing anything with maths while she was taking prep.

"Who did that?" she asked furiously.

"I'm so sorry, Jo," said pretty Anne Seymour. "The books must have been piled too high."

Anne belonged to the Fifth form, and the Fifth were only in here tonight because their own room was in darkness, an electric wire having fused late in the afternoon, so Jo said nothing further.

It remained for Elsie Carr to top off the list of the Middles' iniquities. She had brought back with her one of those absurd animals which when blown up, gradually subside with agonising squawks. Having finished her preparation, Elsie took up her anthology, intending to read poetry for the remaining twenty minutes. Then she felt in her pocket for her handkerchief. It was not there, but the squawker was. With one eye on Jo, who was buried fathoms deep in the life of Molière, Elsie blew him up stealthily. Then she set him on the floor, just at Margia Stevens's feet, and read her book with breathless interest. The squawker set himself to "dying" with an enthusiasm worthy of a better cause, and emitted a heartrending yowl that startled the entire room, at that moment working hard, and fairly silent.

Margia, finishing her harmony, gave a yell, and nearly overturned her desk in the shock of the moment. One or two of the more highly-strung screamed; Cornelia dropped her book, and overbalanced, a natural result of trying to see how long she could stand on one leg. In her fall she grabbed at Joey as the nearest thing handy, and the head girl went with her, nearly overturning the mistress's desk as she fell. A more appalling pandemonium was never heard at the Chalet School.

Into the middle of it irrupted Miss Annersley, and when she had succeeded in gaining silence and finding out the cause of all the disturbance, she read Elsie a lecture that left that young lady gasping and breathless. The punishment which was her reward was a detail after that. She had to lose her breaks for the rest of the week; the squawker was confiscated; she was to do prep with the Juniors over at Le Petit Chalet – also for the rest of the week; and after her prep was finished that night she was to go straight to bed. The bell rang for *Abendessen* in the middle of Miss Annersley's peroration, but she simply carried on till she had finished all she had to say, and the entire room was late in consequence.

Jo, marching upstairs to the prefects' room after the meal was over to try to finish the work that had been so interrupted during prep, voiced her feelings clearly, and the rest of the prefects agreed with her.

"The Middles are very tiresome," said Marie von Eschenau, with a sigh and a thought for the fact that it was *her* turn to take prep the next night. "I wish we might start early-morning prep soon. It is better when the long days come."

"I think so too," agreed Frieda. "Perhaps Mademoiselle will say that next week we may begin."

"There's nothing would make much difference to those Middles!" said Jo – very unjustly, but she had a good deal of work left to do, and had planned to do something else that evening. "They all deserve to be tied up in a sack and dumped into the middle of the lake. At least we'd know where we had them then!"

CHAPTER V

Guides

FOR THE REST OF THE week the Middles appeared to be satisfied with what they had done that night, and there was peace in prep – greatly to the relief of the people who had to take it.

Saturday came, and brought with it the usual Saturday pursuits. From half-past eight till ten they did prep, mending, and letters. At ten, everything was cleared away, and they went for their milk and biscuits. At half-past, came the Guide meeting. The previous Saturday had been taken up with various school activities, so this was the first meeting of term, and they had to decide what badges they would take that term.

"Basket-worker for me," proclaimed Joey that morning, as she was putting on her stockings. "Also, I rather want a shot at Pioneer."

"I will do Basket-worker too," agreed Frieda. "And I should like to take Boatswain, if I may. I have done the Turk's Head, and I know all the knots, and can swim."

"Boatswain wouldn't be bad fun," ruminated Jo. "I think I'll have a shot at it myself. And don't some people intend to take Signaller?"

By the time they were dressed, it had been decided that most of them would do both Basket-worker and Signaller, so they would have to work at their Morse very thoroughly. Downstairs, they found that everyone was eagerly discussing the same subject, and nothing else was talked about during *Frühstück*, rather to the boredom of the staff, who were not all so keen as the girls. Beds were made sketchily that morning, much to the wrath of Matron when she went her rounds. It is on record that seventeen people had to go and remake theirs, and several more found it necessary to get up during the night and tuck themselves in again. Home letters were full of Guide business, and prep was done most casually.

It was left to Cornelia to break the record. Her history exercise, when Miss Stewart – known to the girls as "Charlie" – came to correct it, was a weird mixture of the reign of Elizabeth and Guidework. Part of it ran like this:

Elizabeth was very vain, and keen on Morse. If we work hard, we may get it. Two famous gentlemen at her court were Sir Walter Raleigh and Sir Francis Drake, who sailed round the world, though he knew nothing about wireless. He could not signal if anything happened to him. If Sir Walter Raleigh had known about wireless, he could have told the people in England all about how he was bringing home tobacco, and then his servant would not have thrown water over him, and thought he was burning. You ought not to do this. When a person is on fire, roll them in a rug after you have knocked them down first.

"Charlie", having a keen sense of humour, chuckled over this in private. In public, she told Cornelia that her work was disgraceful, and must be done over again. Cornelia took it quite calmly. Returned lessons were all in the day's work for her, and one more or less made little difference.

When ten o'clock came, everyone was in such a hurry for the meeting that it was only by exercising the strictest vigilance that Matron, who always saw to it on Saturdays, was able to be sure that no girl had missed her milk. The biscuits did not trouble her so much. "They'll be all the hungrier for *Mittagessen*," she reflected philosophically, as girl after girl drained her glass, and then dashed off to join a group, refusing the plain biscuits given them with the milk. But the milk itself was another matter. It was part of the régime instituted by Dr Jem, Dr Mensch, and Dr Maynard of the Sonnalpe, and must be rigidly adhered to. So many of the girls had one or both parents at the sanatorium undergoing treatment, and the doctors were all of the opinion that prevention was infinitely better than cure. "Catch the children early, give them a good foundation, and we may save them," Dr Jem had said on one occasion.

So plenty of milk, sleep, fresh air, and exercise were enforced at the school, and the girls thrived on the treatment.

The day was gloriously fine, for April was going out with laughter, and the sun shone down with vigour. There was a tiny breeze, and the fields were full of early wild flowers.

"It's being a gorgeous spring," said Joey, as she strolled over to join her patrol with Simone Lecoutier, who was Patrol Second in the Carnations.

"I think we shall have an even better summer," assented Simone. "Joey, what about the new girls?"

"What about them?" asked Jo.

"Will they join the Guides?"

"Expect so. Where are they, by the way?"

"Mercy and Faith are with Maria Marani and Hilda Bhaer," replied Simone. "I know nothing about little Gretchen."

"Oh, she'll be with the other Juniors," said Joey easily. "I say! If we have decent weather at half term, won't it be glorious? I'm dying for it to come!"

"It will be very nice," agreed Simone. "I, too, am longing to see the great Passion Play. Who is to play the Christus this year, Joey? Do you know?"

Joey shook her head. "Beyond the fact that it's not Anton Lang – he's a bit on the old side now, after all – I don't know a thing."

"Will Madame let the Robin come with us?" asked Simone.

"Oh, I hope so!" cried Joey. "And Stacie, too. I should think we might rig up some sort of invalid carriage for her, so that she could go. She'll be dying to see it, of course."

"But yes; it is world-famous," observed her friend, as they reached the others, and were straightway plunged into Guide talk, so that the question of the Passion Play was shelved for the time being.

After roll-call, inspection, and drill, Miss Wilson, who was Captain, ordered them to sit on the floor, and then proceeded to question them about badgework. She lifted hands of horror at the list presented to her, and set to work to cut it up at once. "You can't possibly do all this, girls," she said. "No one may take more than three badges, and I see that some of you are down for four and five. You must think it out, and decide what you will drop. I'll give you five minutes now, and please be sensible about it."

"But, Miss *Wilson!*" protested Jo.

"Bill" proved adamant, however. "You have your schoolwork as well, Jo, and this is the hot-weather term. There will be the excitement of Oberammergau at half-term, and you can't possibly do all this and keep fit. I'm sorry, but you must do as I said."

Jo pulled a face and sat down again, to discuss with Frieda which was the more important badge for them – Pioneer or Boatswain. They finally decided to drop Pioneer, for if they left Boatswain this term, it must mean waiting till next summer, as it was essentially a summer badge. The lake was frozen over for five months or so during the winter, and would not be available for work. Apart from that, the sudden storms that swept down on it through the narrow mountain passes rendered it dangerous for the girls during the spring and autumn, and the authorities would never hear of steady work on it once the autumn had set in.

When finally the list had been adjusted to something more in keeping with "Bill's" ideas on the subject, she turned to talk of something she had very much at heart.

"You all know that St Scholastika's has started Guides this term, girls?" she said. "I want you to extend a helping hand to them. We are an old company in comparison with them; we have several Guides with the all-round cord, and several who hold the first-class badge. They are all novices in the movement, and I want you to help them – tactfully, of course – as much as ever you can. To that end, Miss Browne and Mademoiselle have arranged that this term you shall go camping together at the weekends, as soon as the weather permits. Two patrols from each company will go every weekend, with the exception of the Oberammergau week. You will go in strict rotation, and while in camp you will be expected to give a helping hand to the new Guides, so that they may be able to catch up with us as far as possible."

She paused here, and a buzz of comment ran round the listening girls. Camping was something all had wanted, but it had been difficult to arrange before this. For one thing, none of the Guiders had held a camper's licence. Luckily Miss Stewart, who had been new the previous term, held hers, so that difficulty was now overcome. Then, while the Chalet company had been new, Mrs Russell had hesitated over taking them out. Now, however, they were experienced, and would be able to help the members of St Scholastika's, the other school on the lake-side.

"Camping *and* the Passion Play!" cried Margia Stevens ecstatically when they were at liberty to talk once more. "Oh! What a gorgeous term this is going to be!"

In saying this she only voiced the feelings of everyone. Even quiet Frieda was flushed and excited, while Jo was so thrilled that she forgot her position as head girl, and summed up her feelings in one forbidden word. "*Golloptious!*" she said.

"It was a splendid idea of Madame's to send us to the Passion Play," said Marie earnestly. "To have camping added to that – well, it strikes me that we are having the time of our lives."

"How Gisela and Wanda and Bernhilda and Grizel will wish they were here now!" added Simone.

"Grizel *is* going to the Passion Play," said Jo. "I had a letter from her this morning, and she says she's going to try to arrange it at the same time as us."

"Could Grizel not come here and go with us?" asked Frieda eagerly.

"Frieda! What a great idea! Of course she must! I'll write tomorrow, and tell her she's got to!"

The shrilling blast of Miss Wilson's whistle broke across their rejoicing, and they came to attention at once, to find that she wanted them to form up for a march out. The four girls going up to the Sonnalpe for the weekend would be excused, so that they might go and get ready, as Dr Maynard would arrive for them shortly. Joey, Marie, Evadne, and little Irma von Rothenfels, one of the Robin's special chums, saluted and ran off to change into afternoon frocks, and get on their berets and coats, while the rest formed in line, and, led by the Carnations, marched out of the big school-room, down the path, and off round the lake to Seespitz. The Brownies had their own march towards the great Tiern Pass, for the Guides meant to go to Seehof on the other side of the lake, and this was too far for their small legs.

"And Dr Maynard will have to carry Irma," declared Jo, as they stood in the hall waiting for him.

"Me, I can walk quite well, Joey," declared Irma, deeply insulted at this suggestion. "I am not a baby – no."

"You'll be glad to be carried," said Joey calmly. "It's an awful pull, Irma. I shouldn't mind being carried myself, sometimes."

Irma shook her small head till the long, dark pigtails wagged furiously behind her. "I am not a baby," she repeated.

Jo grinned, but made no other reply. She knew quite well that the small girl would be thankful for Dr Maynard's strong arms before they had reached the halfway point up the Sonnalpe. Marie and Evadne, who had been up before, repeated the grin. Lazy Evadne went further. "I just wish I was kid enough to be carried," she said feelingly. "Gee! Your back an' legs do ache after it!"

"You aren't allowed to say 'gee'," Joey reminded her. "And if you weren't so awfully lazy you'd keep in better trim, and then you wouldn't mind it."

Evadne put out her tongue at her, but Jo was in holiday mood and, into the bargain, had forgotten that she was a prefect, much less head girl, so the little

American escaped the Nemesis she deserved. It is true Marie looked rather shocked, but as Jo took no notice, she saw no reason why she should interfere. Luckily, before anything worse occurred, Dr Maynard put in an appearance, and demanded that they should set off at once. He had been in Innsbruck since the Wednesday and was anxious to get back. He gave Irma no option in the matter, but scooped her up, and set her on his shoulder. Then, taking the big case that held the belongings of all four girls, he bade the others "Trot!", and they set forth for a jolly weekend.

CHAPTER VI

On the Sonnalpe

THE LITTLE STEAMERS THAT TAKE passengers across the lake during the season were not yet running, so the girls, led by the young doctor, went round the shore to Seespitz, and then cut across the water meadows to Maurach, a hamlet on the other side of the railway. Here was the chalet belonging to the Maranis, where they came to spend the summer months. It was closed as yet, but Joey, as they passed it, remarked to Marie that it would be opened in another week or so. "Tante Gisel and Onkel Florian are coming early this year, as Tante Gisel wants to be near Gisela and Baby Natalie," she said.

"I can understand that," replied Marie. "Oh, Joey! I *am* so longing to see Gisela and the baby! Only think; she is the first grandchild the Chalet School has!"

Joey chuckled. "So she is. I hadn't thought of that. Aren't we coming on?"

"Guess there aren't many schools our age have grandchildren," said Evadne proudly. "Maria is tickled to death that she's an aunt."

"Well, to be an aunt at thirteen isn't bad," agreed Jo. "*I* was fourteen when the twins arrived."

"And I can't ever be an aunt," sighed Evadne, who was an only child.

"Yes, you can, if you marry someone with dozens of sisters and brothers and they have children," said Jo cheerfully.

"Oh, *that*!" Evadne sounded scornful.

"Well, you *might*. You never know. – Here we are at last!"

They had reached the foot of the narrow path that leads up the Sonnalpe and stood waiting till the doctor came up with them. He set Irma down, and suggested that they should call at the little *Gasthaus* nearby for coffee. "It won't take many minutes, and it'll be late enough for *Mittagessen* when we get there," he said. "Come along, girls. We've time enough for that."

He led the way into the *Speisesaal*, where a sturdily-built girl in short skirt and tight bodice, with flaxen hair braided tightly back from her face, served them with the milky coffee and twists of sweet bread they all loved. The girls were hungry and enjoyed the little meal. Jo was the first to finish, and while the rest were still busy she leant back in her chair. A group at the table in the opposite window attracted her attention, and she leant towards Marie, whispering excitedly, "I say, there's those people that came up with us and stared so at us. They must be staying here."

Marie turned and looked. "So it is! But it is early for visitors, Jo."

"What's that?" asked the doctor, who had caught her last remark.

"Those people over there," said Jo, nodding in their direction. "They came up with us from Innsbruck when we came—"

"*We!* I was under the impression that *you* came from the Sonnalpe," laughed the doctor.

"Well, you know what I mean. I saw them when I met the others, anyway, and Frieda said that they had come up from Innsbruck, and simply stared all the way. I wonder why they're here? They don't look as if they had anyone up at the san, and it's early for visitors yet."

"That's no reason why they shouldn't come, all the same," returned the doctor. "You haven't bought up the lake-side, Joey!"

Jo laughed. "I know that. Don't be silly, Dr Jack! Only it *is* early for visitors – unless they have a reason."

He did not dispute her remark, for he knew what she meant. The Sonnalpe with its population of sufferers was very near the girls. Elsie Carr, Anne Seymour, Violet Allison, Signa Johansen, and many others were at the school because someone in their family was in the big sanatorium. And the Chalet School was responsible for three beds in the children's free ward. Frieda's brother, Madge's husband – himself the brother of a former mistress – all formed links with the school. It would have been strange if the girls had not felt the Sonnalpe and its shadows very near to them.

Now he turned his attention to the party. Two ladies and a tall gentleman made it up. The ladies he did not know; but at sight of the man his face suddenly lit up, and he got to his feet with a hasty exclamation. "Hillis! What a surprise! My dear chap, I thought you were still in the Antipodes!"

The stranger looked up in surprise, which changed to a smile as he sprang to his feet, holding out his hand. "Maynard, by all that's wonderful! What on earth are you doing here?"

Dr Maynard waved his hand towards the Sonnalpe,

which could be seen through the window. "I'm at the sanatorium up there. I called at the school to collect some of the girls for the weekend."

"By Jove! But this is a shock! The school, you say? Do you mean the wonderful Chalet School of which we have been hearing so much? My mother and wife have been awfully interested in both it and St Scholastika's. By the way, Dr Maynard – my mother, and my wife."

They remained for a little, chatting. Mrs Hillis senior was a charming woman who had spent nearly all her life abroad. Little Mrs Frank Hillis was an Irish girl, whose first visit abroad this was. The doctor called his charges over to them, and introduced them, and Jo, with all her usual lack of shyness, was soon chattering away at top speed, ably seconded by Evadne, while Marie put in shy remarks occasionally, and small Irma replied to little Mrs Frank's petting. The two men exchanged news, and then the doctor glanced at his watch. "Time we were getting on, you people. They will wonder what has happened if we are late. Get your traps, and come along. – Sorry to rush off like this, Hillis, but I'm due back there now, and we've a stiff walk before us."

The girls, all well trained to instant obedience, collected their belongings, and were soon ready to set off.

"You must come up and see us soon," said the doctor, as they said goodbye. "It's a pull; but not too bad, and we have a glorious view from the alm, once you get there. And I want you to meet my chief, Hillis – Russell, you know. He's Joey's brother-in-law, and one of the best. And there's two or three other folk up there too. Come up next week and spend a week with us. There's room at the hotel just now."

The elder Mrs Hillis smiled. "It would be very nice. We can manage it, I should think. But Frank will write and let you know, Dr Maynard, what we decide."

"Good!" said the doctor. "I hope you will come. – Now then, you people, are you ready? – Up you get,

Irma. – Evadne, don't start hanging on to someone so soon. I'll give you a hand when we get to the worst place, but you are not to hang on to either Jo or Marie. They will have enough to do to look after themselves. – Goodbye, Mrs Hillis – goodbye, Mrs Frank – so long, old man!"

He swept his little party away, leaving the newcomers waving goodbye to them, and the five set off up the path, which twisted through grass meadows at first. Presently they came to clumps of pine trees which grew in number, till finally they were going through the pine forest, where the air was warm and delicious with the scent of the trees, and the sun shone through in places, dappling the pine-needle-covered ground with patches of gold. This was easy going, though Evadne the lazy complained of the gradient. "I loathe climbing," she said. "Why don't they make a proper road for autos?"

"There is one at the other end," said Jo.

"I guess there is. Half the sick folk couldn't get up here if there weren't. But that's not our end."

"Well, it won't kill you to walk for once," said Jo heartlessly. "Work some of the fat off you."

Evadne uttered a squeal of rage. "I'm *not* fat! Jo Bettany, you're a – a—" she suddenly dried up as she caught the doctor's eye. Evadne's language was picturesque on occasion, though her years at the Chalet School had cured her of some of the more outrageous expressions. Still, as Mademoiselle Lepâttre had remarked on one occasion, there was never any knowing what she would say next.

Jo was merciful for once – besides, she was finding that she needed all her breath for the climb, so she refrained from further teasing, and they went on in silence till they had got beyond the rim of the forest and reached another grassy stretch, where the green of the turf was starred with the bright colours of the early flowers.

Here grew gentian and narcissi, wild heartsease and crocus, and many another lovely blossom. The doctor amiably set Irma down so that she might gather a nosegay to take to "Madame". He would allow very little pausing, for the afternoon was getting on, and the girls had not had a proper meal since *Frühstück*, early in the morning; but Irma got her flowers with some assistance from the other three, and then he swung her up again, and they went on.

Now they had left the grass, and come to the worst part – a narrow, rocky path, through boulders of limestone, with only occasional patches of moss or lichen to liven up the scene. Halfway up Joey paused, to turn and gaze down on the valley lying below them. The lake, blue in the afternoon sunshine, gleamed like a jewel, and the hamlets scattered round it looked like the toys of some giant child, tossed here and there at random. Opposite them were the mighty peaks of the Bärenbad Alpe, the Mondscheinspitz, the Tiernjoch, and Bärenkopf, white beneath the sunlight. Away to the north they could see blue hills fading into the blue of the sky. To the south lay other and mightier peaks, some still covered with snow, silent testimony to their height.

"Come on, Joey!" said the doctor at length. "We shall never get there at this rate. You and Marie take the bag between you – and Evadne, come and hold on to my arm. This is the worst bit."

They did as they were told, and the next twenty minutes held some quite strenuous climbing. There was no danger, but it was hard work, and when they had finally emerged from the boulder-strewn part, and were once more on the grass, they were thankful to pause to wipe their streaming faces. However, very little more remained of the mountain path, and once they had reached the alm they found Dr Jem there with his little car, waiting to take them to Die Rosen and Madge, and a good meal.

"You've been slow," he said, as he packed them in.

"Well, between Joey's star-gazing and Irma's flower-gathering, can you wonder?" demanded his colleague. "Things all right over there?" He indicated the great sanatorium with a nod of his head.

Dr Jem frowned. "Tell you everything later," he said. "The first thing to do is to get these kids to a good meal."

He glanced at Jo's white face and heavy eyes as he spoke. Much stronger than they had ever hoped she would be, she was far from robust, and she tired easily. Marie, too, looked very weary and ready for something.

Apart from that, there was bad news at the sanatorium, and the doctor wanted the girls to have a meal before they heard it. They all knew and liked Mr Eastley, the Protestant chaplain at the school. He had come out to be with his wife, a frail little woman who had been ill for some months. She had died quite happily the day before, in her husband's arms. Marie and Jo and Evadne had all known her, and he knew that they would be upset. Luckily, they had not noticed either Dr Maynard's question or his own look, and they reached Die Rosen in happy ignorance of the sad facts. Madge was at the door to welcome them, David in her arms; and Gisela and Baby Natalie were in the big salon with the Robin and the Bettany twins, two jolly little people nearly three years old. There was someone else there, too. Lying in an invalid chair, which had come from Vienna only the day before, was Stacie, and at sight of her the girls forgot everything else and inundated her with questions.

"Stacie! When did you get downstairs?"

"Stacie! But this is splendid! I did not know you were so much better!"

"Say, Stacie, old thing, how long have you been here?"

Stacie, a slight, fair girl, with keen grey eyes, and a faint flush of excitement in cheeks normally pale, laughed. "Madame sent to Vienna for this chair, and Dr

Jem and Dr Mensch lifted me into it after *Mittagessen* today, and brought me down in the lift. I am to use it every day. And see: when I can be raised, there is a spring here which lifts it little by little. I am up four inches today, and they think I may be raised another inch in a fortnight's time. It all depends, of course, on how my back goes on. And I am to be wheeled out in it tomorrow afternoon if it is fine."

"Gorgeous!" declared Jo. "We shall have you back at school in half no time at this rate."

"And now," said Madge, "you people must go and make yourselves fit to be seen. – I suppose you know your hair is more like a golliwog's than ever, Jo? Evadne looks as if she has rubbed her face and hands on every tree trunk she has met, and even Marie is untidy. – That's something fresh for you, Marie! – Come with me, Irma, and Robin and I will take you up to the room you are sharing with her. – Joey, I have put Marie in your room, and Evadne shares with Stacie. Show her where to go. Trot, all of you! What is it, Peggy, baba?"

Peggy, a tiny girl, with fair curls running over her little head, and big, appealing blue eyes, was pulling at her aunt's frock. "Me come, too," she pleaded.

"Come along, then. – Rix, you come, too. Then I shall know where you are."

They left the room, and Madge, walking first with Jo and Marie one on each side of her, said in an undertone, "Rix is an imp of mischief. There's never any knowing what he's up to except when he's asleep. He has all the original sin of himself and Peggy. She is as good as gold, except when he drags her into his misdeeds."

"I see you having some fun when David is old enough to join them," laughed Jo. "What a time you will have!"

"Jem will take him in hand," returned Jem's wife confidently. "Besides, I am going to get a 'Mam'selle' for them. Three babies and the Robin and Stacie are more than I can manage."

"Don't tell me the Robin is a handful, for I shan't believe it."

"No; but she needs very great care."

They had reached the upper corridor by this time, and the babies and Evadne had vanished into their rooms. Madge turned to Marie. "Go and help Irma, Marie dear. Jo will tell you later what I am going to tell her."

"Yes, of course, Madame," said Marie, dropping the curtsy that was always insisted on at the Chalet School.

She followed the small people into the Robin's pretty room, and the two sisters went on to the bigger one which belonged to Jo. That young lady tossed her beret and coat on the bed, and then faced her sister. "Madge! There's nothing wrong with the Robin?"

Madge shook her head slowly. "Hard to say, Joey. You know what we have always feared for her—"

A cry from Jo interrupted her. "Madge! Not that for the Robin!"

Madge's lips trembled. "Jo, we can't say – yet. She tires easily, and her breathing is very short—"

"That's always been her trouble," interrupted Jo.

"I know. Darling, Jem and Jack Maynard and Gottfried Mensch are being very careful – very watchful. She has everything in her favour up here. But – there are symptoms they don't like. She seems to get a little fever as the evening goes on; and she *is* very breathless at times. They hope it may just be the outcome of her growth. She is growing very quickly just now. There is no cough, and they say her lungs are quite sound. But there is a weakness – and her mother died of it. The Robin will not go back to school now until she is fourteen at least. Jem says that even if they succeed in saving her from this, she must be where she can be in the hands of doctors for the next four or five years, and where can she be better than here?"

Jo turned away to hide the tears in her black eyes. The

Robin was as dear to her as her own sister, and she knew – for they had told her long ago – how frail was the little girl's hold on life. The pretty Polish mother who had died while the Robin was little more than a baby had bequeathed to her tiny daughter her own delicate constitution, and only the unceasing care and love she had had could have brought her through even as far as she had come. If this dread were to come true – Joey knew what little strength there was to battle against it.

Madge got up from her seat on the bed, and came over to her. "Joey, it hasn't come yet. They are taking the utmost care. Herr Schiedmann of Vienna is coming here in a fortnight to discuss some new treatment with the doctors here. Jem will ask him to examine her, and if he can tell us of anything further to do, it will be done. Remember; it hasn't begun yet. There is the fear of it; but only the fear so far."

"Uncle Ted?"

Madge's face shadowed at this mention of the Robin's father. "Yes; he knows. Joey, remember I have trusted you. Robin knows nothing about it, of course; nor do we want anyone else to know except Marie – and you may tell Frieda. Evvy is too young, and the others don't feel about her as we do."

"Juliet?" questioned Jo, naming her sister's ward, who was like another sister to her and the Robin.

"Juliet must know. She worships the Robin, and I couldn't keep her in ignorance. But you are to tell no one else. After all, we are hoping it may pass, and she may grow as healthy as you have done. Jem thinks we shall know very soon which it is. There is one good thing in her favour. She has not lost her appetite, and that is all to the good."

Jo nodded, and went to the dressing-table, where she stood brushing her thick mop with swift, mechanical strokes. Madge watched her for a moment; then, divining that she would prefer to be alone, rose quietly and went to see what the small people were doing. As soon as she had gone, Jo tossed her brush down anywhere, and went to kneel at the window. For a long time she knelt there, staring with unseeing eyes at the wonderful panorama of mountain peaks spread before her. Suddenly she broke down and, laying her head down on her outstretched arms, wept the bitterest tears she had ever shed.

CHAPTER VII

The Robin

How LONG SHE LAY THERE sobbing Jo never knew. It seemed hours, though it was, as a matter of fact, barely twenty minutes. Then a hand was laid on her shoulders, and Marie's soft voice exclaimed tenderly, "But Joey, my dear! Tell me what is wrong."

Jo kept her head down, and she still shook with the violence of her outburst. Tears were foreign to her, and crying hurt her badly. This had been an unusual breakdown for her, and not all at once could she control herself. Marie, wise with the wisdom of affection, sat down beside her and said nothing, though she patted her chum's shoulder from time to time.

Presently Jo contrived to get hold of herself. The tears ceased, and though she still quivered with sobs she was able to speak. Without raising her head, she said gruffly, "How did you get here?"

"Madame sent me," replied Marie.

Jo shifted her arms till they rested on Marie's knee,

and stayed quiet for a moment. Then she spoke again. "Did she – tell you – anything?"

"Nothing. What is it, Joey? Can't I help?"

"I don't see how anyone can. It's the Robin," came in muffled tones from Marie's knee.

"The Robin?"

"Yes. They – are – afraid—"

Joey could get no further. Not yet could she frame the words that might mean so terribly much to them all. Marie, however, knew, like the rest of the elder girls, what was to be feared, and she guessed at once. Her arms tightened round Joey, and she laid her cheek against the rough black head. "Oh, Joey! Not that – not that for the Robin!"

"They're afraid," said Jo briefly.

There was a little silence. The tears were in Marie's violet eyes, and her lovely face was flushed. She had remained with the younger children, taking them downstairs again after Irma had made herself presentable, and staying with them till Madge, who had run along to the nursery with David, came back to them. She had at once seen the shadow on the beloved face of the ex-Head, and had wondered very much when "Madame" had said to her, "Run along up to Joey, Marie. She wants you."

Marie had run upstairs, a faint, indefinable dread stirring at her heart. But she had not imagined anything like this. Sitting there, her arms round Jo, she recalled the Robin's appearance as it had first struck her this afternoon. Could it be true that the little girl had seemed frailer?

She had reached this point when Joey moved, and lifted her head. "Marie!"

At once Marie bent over her friend. "What is it, *Herzliebchen*?"

"They – they aren't sure – yet. It may just be that she is growing too quickly."

"She *is* growing very quickly," said Marie, a faint hope

dawning in her eyes. "Joey! It may just be that."

"They are going to ask – some man from Vienna when he comes next week," went on Jo in monotonous tones which betrayed how fragile was her self-control. "He is awfully clever, and knows most of what is to be known about – *it*. But anyhow, it's going to mean that she must stay here for the next few years. She – won't be coming down to school now till she is fourteen or fifteen years old."

"But you will have finished school then," said Marie soothingly. "You will be here with her, Jo. Oh, but aren't you going to Elisaveta next year?"

"Not if there's anything badly wrong with the Robin," returned Jo. "Veta wouldn't ask it. And if she did, it wouldn't make any difference if she were fifty times the Crown Princess."

"Veta won't ask," agreed Marie, her thoughts going swiftly to the little Crown Princess of Belsornia who, for two happy terms, had been just an ordinary schoolgirl at the Chalet School in the days when she and Joey had been Middles, and the Robin a roly-poly baby whom everyone adored.

The Crown Princess Elisaveta was too important a person, once she stood on the steps of the throne, to be allowed to continue this free and easy life. She must go home to Belsornia and learn all the many things necessary for a future queen to learn, which are not taught in ordinary schools. But she and Joey had always been chums, and it had been arranged that when Jo was eighteen, she was to go to Belsornia as lady-in-waiting to the Princess. In many countries this could not have been done; but the Belsornians are a democratic race and, in any case, Jo had helped to save their little Princess from the hands of her father's cousin, a wicked schemer, Prince Cosimo, who at that time had been heir to the throne after the present King Carol, then Crown Prince. That episode had ended in Cosimo's breaking his neck down a ravine near the Tiern Pass, and the end of the Salic Law in Belsornia, so that the Princess might be her father's heir. The Belsornians all worshipped the Little Lady of Belsornia, as they named the child, and Jo, since she had saved her from what might have been a terrible fate, was almost second in their hearts. So there would be no difficulty there when – or *if* – Joey took up her duties at the court.

"Veta won't ask you to leave the Robin, Joey," said Marie tenderly. "She wants you, I know; but she, too, loves the Robin."

"We all do that." Joey had pulled herself together, and though her shoulders still heaved with an occasional sob, she had stopped crying. She sat on the floor, one arm still on Marie's knee, her black eyes gazing out over the mountains.

"And it isn't definite," went on Marie in her soft voice, which made music of the guttural German they were both speaking. "It may be that she is growing so quickly. She is getting very tall, you know, and she is only ten."

"It was last term's upset when we were at Fulpmes that has done this," said Joey. Suddenly she twisted round to face her friend. "Marie, if – if anything happens, I shall never forgive Eustacia – *never*!"

"You mustn't talk like that now, Joey."

"I mean it, though. The long hours of worry when we were all away upset her badly, and it will be that that has started this."

But Marie was able to see more clearly than Jo for once. "Joey, if it is – as they fear – it only means that sooner or later it must have come. But I won't believe it," she added. "Everyone has always taken such care of the Robin. She has had every chance, and she will have more now. Joey, if it *should* be, then it can only mean that nothing could have saved it."

Jo turned away, a hard look in her face. "I shall know whom to blame," was all she said.

Marie looked troubled. This was a Jo she had never seen before, and she had no idea how to deal with her. She got to her feet and brought Jo's brush. "Let me put your hair tidy," she said coaxingly. "Then, if you wash your face and hands, we can go downstairs. *Kaffee* must be nearly finished, and the little ones will be wondering where we are."

Jo submitted to having her mop brushed, and then went to the bathroom, where she contrived to clear her face of tearstains. When finally she was ready they went downstairs together, but she was a subdued Jo, and one who refused to look or speak directly to Stacie, who lay on her couch watching her with anxious eyes. Eustacia had known that Jo must blame her and she could scarcely expect anything else in the circumstances. Nevertheless she watched the elder girl with wistful eyes that begged for forgiveness for that fit of temper on the glacier during the previous term which had resulted in Miss Wilson's being lamed and the detention of the whole party in the *Alpenhütte* for the whole night. The worry the Robin had undergone during those hours when her beloved Joey had never returned had told on a constitution naturally frail, and the child had never been the same since. More deeply than ever did Stacie wish that she had managed to control herself on that fatal afternoon.

Meanwhile, Jo herself had eyes for little but the Robin. When Irma would have a romp, Jo stopped it by offering to tell stories to the little ones. She was famed in the school for her stories, and Robin and Irma at once rushed to her and tumbled down beside her. Jo stooped and pulled the Robin up to her lap, where she nursed her during the hour that followed. Peggy and Rix were abstracted early, and marched off to bed by an inflexible nurse, who came later for the two little girls. Jo carried her treasure upstairs, and Madge made no protest for once.

"Put me to bed yourself, Joey," pleaded the Robin.

"Rather!" said Jo. "There won't be any playing about,

though. Just prayers and bath and bed, and then I'll tuck you in, and sing till you go to sleep."

"*Nice!*" sighed the Robin, beaming with content.

Jo kept her word. She waited till the small girl had said her prayers and then whisked her off to the bathroom, where she bathed her, and dried her, and tucked her into her warm pyjamas before bearing her back to the pretty room she was to share with Irma for this weekend. Irma was already in bed, for Rosa, the nurse, had been quicker than Jo. She squealed with delight when she saw the Robin, and then Joey dropped her burden on to the bed, and proceeded to tuck her up very thoroughly. "Now, lie still, both of you, and close your eyes," she commanded. "I'm going to sing to you, and I promise not to leave till you are asleep."

Both snuggled down, and long lashes swept rose-flushed cheeks. Joey, with a little pang to see how frail the Robin looked beside sturdy Irma, curled up at the foot of her darling's little bed, and sang in a voice which had the ethereal quality of a chorister's the Robin's favourite lullaby, 'The Red Sarafan'. It was a Russian song, and the pretty Polish mother, who had died five years before this, had never failed to rock her little daughter to sleep with it till the last fortnight before her death. The Robin loved it, and had insisted that Jo should learn it with the same phrasing and turns as her mother had used. Madge and Marie, listening in the salon below, with Evadne, subdued by the unusual atmosphere and playing halma with Stacie, listened with tears in their eyes, as there were tears in Jo's voice. When the song was ended it was followed by a barcarolle; then the 'Shepherd's Cradle-Song' of Arthur Somervell. Jo sang it exquisitely, the golden notes filling the quiet house with a magic that sent the servants about their work on tiptoe, and silenced even Evadne's comments. There was silence when it came to an end; then the sound of quiet footsteps, and the careful closing of a door.

Joey appeared in the salon ten minutes later, and settled down with a book for the rest of the evening.

Only when Stacie was wheeled away to her room, Evadne following, she barely lifted her head to reply to the wistful, "Goodnight, Joey."

"Oh, going, are you?" she said carelessly. "Goodnight, then."

"Night, old thing," said Evadne. "Sleep tight!"

"Goodnight, Evvy. Don't talk in your sleep, if you can help it!"

Then the two younger girls vanished, and there were left only the doctor and his wife, Captain Humphries, Marie, and Jo. Captain Humphries got up presently and murmured something about letters. He left the room, and Jo flung down the book, not one page of which had she read properly. "Jem," she said, "we want to know everything."

The doctor lit his pipe, and frowned at the flowers on a nearby table in silence. Then he turned to the girl. "There is little to tell, Joey," he said quietly. "There is no disease – *so far as we can judge* – at present. But there *is* a very strong predisposition to it; and I don't like this breathlessness, nor the way in which she tires. Herr Schiedmann will examine her when he comes and give us his considered opinion. He is very clever, and will not miss anything. Until then we can do nothing but watch her, and hope. Whatever you do, girls, don't lose hope. She will have every chance, for she will have every care that love and science can give her."

"But – what do you think yourself, Jem?" asked Joey insistently.

"Honestly, Jo, I don't know. I don't like the temperature – but lots of excitable children run temperatures for no obvious reason, and it doesn't mean this thing we dread. She hasn't lost weight as yet – or very little. She is eating well, and she has no cough. I am pinning my faith to those things. Try not to worry too much, Jo. I hope it is just a false alarm. But we agreed to tell you because we knew how you would feel if the worst happened and we left you to find out for yourself. Look here, Jo, old girl, it's not too late in the evening yet. You and Marie run and get something on, and we four will walk down and see Gisela. She was here when you came, but she had to go away almost at once, and saw scarcely anything of you. Trot, the three of you!"

They went off to don coats and berets, and presently all four were walking down to Das Pferd, where Gisela sat sewing by the lamp, and Gottfried was reading some learned tome, which he put down gladly enough when the visitors were announced.

When they were all sitting quietly, Gisela hearing the latest news of her old friend Wanda from Marie, and Mrs Russell listening to the talk, Jo turned to Dr Mensch. "Gottfried, what do *you* think of the Robin? I've heard what Jem has to say. I want to know what *you* think."

He laid down his china-bowled pipe, and looked at her doubtfully. "So they have told you, *Mädchen*?"

"Of course. You don't suppose Madge would keep me in the dark about a thing like that?"

"No; perhaps not."

"Well, what do you think?"

He shook his head. "I cannot say, yet. There is the fear that disease may develop, but that is all so far."

"And you've always known that, Joey," added her brother-in-law.

"I've always known it – yes. But nothing so – so *near* as this."

"It seems nearer now, I admit," said Dr Mensch, taking up his pipe again. "But till Schiedmann has seen her and given us his opinion, I must refuse to make any statement. She is not strong; and she is not well at present. That is the most any of us can say. She is sound enough so far. The dear God grant that it may continue."

"How d'you know?" demanded Jo.

"We examined her this morning," replied Jem quietly. "Don't fret, Jo, she will be watched like a baby queen. Better, even; for we know what there is to fear, and we are prepared for it. If it be within our power, the trouble will never get any hold on her."

Gottfried got up. "Bring thy violin, *mein Liebling*," he said to his wife. "Let us have some music. Joey shall sing for us; and thou shalt play."

Nor would he allow any further discussion, and the evening was pleasantly passed in music. Jo sang very little, but they were merciful and let her alone. Gisela and Marie both played the violin well, and Gottfried himself was a fine performer. Madge could play their accompaniments, and Dr Russell owned a pleasant baritone. It was late, and the moon was up when they finally left for home, walking through "a wonderful clear night of stars", Joey went a little apart, her delicate face upturned to the myriad worlds that twinkled above them. The others took no notice of her, and when she knelt down at the window-sill to say her prayers, and stayed there for long, Marie made no comment. She knew that Jo was asking of the great Father the Robin's happy little life.

CHAPTER VIII

A Chapter of Accidents

THAT WAS A VERY QUIET weekend. Jo could not forget the Robin's danger. She could not find any comfort in the company of her sister or her friends, knowing how anxious they all were. The only comfort she found was not from any human being. Rufus, her big St Bernard, now living at Die Rosen since Madge's marriage, had greeted Joey with joy, but the moment she spoke to him he knew that something was wrong, and in the wonderful way dogs have he tried to comfort her. He eyed her anxiously, nosed her and whimpered softly as he licked her. Joey, burying her face in his deep coat, knew that here was someone who, not understanding why, yet knew she was unhappy and was determined to show how much he loved her. His devotion helped Joey to endure one of the worst weekends of her life.

Evadne woke up on the Sunday morning with a swollen cheek, and had to be soothed most of the day with chilli paste and lotion for a tooth that should have received attention at least a month before. She scorned tears, but they weren't far off, and she was glad to spend the afternoon lying down on the couch in the salon, the poor cheek well smothered in paste, and her head swathed in flannel. Towards evening the pain went away, and the swelling began to go down. But Dr Jem insisted that a visit to the dentist must be paid that week, and Evadne had a horror of Herr von Francius and all his works. "Aw, let it go. The pain's gone," she implored the doctor.

He shook his head. "No use, Evvy. That tooth is a poison-trap as long as it's in your mouth in its present condition. I shall see Mademoiselle tomorrow when I take you people down, and shall tell her that I am going to carry you off to Innsbruck straight away. I have to go to meet Herr Schiedmann anyway, so we might as well get it all over at once."

"Well, say I tell him to take it out and be done with it?" she pleaded.

"That will lie with him. Personally, I expect he will stop it. It isn't so badly gone as all that."

Evadne flung away from him. "You're *mean*, Dr Jem!"

she cried wrathfully. "You *know* how I hate that—"

She caught his eye, and suddenly stopped. Certain words and phrases were strictly forbidden to her, and she knew it. The doctor chuckled. "'Discretion is the better part of valour,' eh, Evvy? Never mind; you probably won't have half such a bad time as you expect. When it's all over we'll have some fun. The Vienna–Paris express doesn't arrive till four o'clock, so we shall have most of the morning and all the afternoon before us."

Evadne refused to be consoled, however, and stalked off, leaving him laughing.

Eustacia, knowing how much she might be to blame over the trouble with the Robin, relapsed into one of her old-time silences, and read industriously most of the day. If anyone had asked her what she had been reading, however, she would have been puzzled to reply. As for the two little ones, and the three babies, they were taken for a walk in the morning, spent the afternoon in a siesta, and then were read to after *Kaffee*, till Madge, with the aid of Jo and Marie, put them to bed at six o'clock.

Monday morning saw the four schoolgirls and the doctor going down the mountain path very early. Since they were now in May, it was far warmer than it had been on the day when Jo had gone back to school, and by the time they reached the lake they were all hot. Jo eyed the blue waters longingly. "Wish we could bathe," she said.

"Not yet," returned the doctor. "But there's Herr Weisen in his boat. Give him a yell, Joey, and we'll get him to row us across."

Jo lifted her voice in a long, musical yodel, and the solitary fisher on the lake, recognizing it, pulled in his line and rowed across to them. He readily consented to row them to the little landing-stage opposite the school, and they tumbled into the boat gaily.

"We'll be early," said Jo, as she sat trailing her hand in the water. "This is quicker than going round."

"Much pleasanter, too," agreed Marie. Then she

withdrew her fingers from the water with a little shiver. "Brrr! But the water still remains cold! I should not like to bathe yet."

"No; I don't think I should really," said Jo. "That's the worst of these spring-fed lakes. They generally are as cold as Christmas!"

Marie laughed, and glanced across at Evadne, who sat in the stern of the boat, Irma beside her, her face very doleful. "Cheer up, Evadne! It cannot last long, and then Dr Jem will give you a good time."

"It's easy to talk!" growled Evadne. "'Tisn't *you* has to go through with it. Guess if it was, you wouldn't be so cheery over it."

"Don't be an ass!" said Jo heartlessly. "It's not like you to funk, Evvy. Pull up your socks, and don't be so soft!"

Evadne snarled, but said nothing coherent, so they let her alone, and a minute later were drawing up to the boat-slip. The doctor sprang out, lifted out the younger girls, and gave a hand to the other two. Then he slipped a couple of schillings into the boatman's hand, sending him off chuckling at his good fortune, and walked his party up to the school. *Frühstück* was ready for them when they arrived, and when it was over he and Evadne set off to catch the little train that ran down the mountainside to Spärtz, while the other three went into school, agreeably conscious that they had managed to miss the best part of the first lesson.

Stationery was always given out during Break on Monday mornings, and Frieda went to the cupboard, a huge affair like a small room, as soon as history was ended. The stationery monitresses of each form came with lists which had to be signed by the form mistress, and Frieda's duty consisted in giving out what was required on the lists, which she then signed and returned, so that they might go to the mistress concerned for checking. In addition, the inkwell monitresses came before school on Mondays, and she had to fill their ink-cans for them. The Juniors had their own stationery, over at Le Petit Chalet, and their wants were attended to by their own mistress. Frieda, careful and methodical, was a very good stationery prefect, and she got through the work well and quickly. It was still near enough to the beginning of term for few of the girls to need more than notebooks or pen nibs.

However, on this occasion Miss Wilson had demanded that the Third should do their maps on drawing-paper and, when they were done, paste them into their geography books. Drawing was not a strong point with the Third, and she had suffered much with maps drawn on paper that had had all the surface rubbed off. Painted maps came out all smeary and indistinct as a result of this, and the geography books were a sight to behold. "You children can do your maps first, and put them in your books afterwards," she said at the last lesson. "But remember, you may have no more than three pieces of paper at a time. You ought not to need *that*, but your work is simply disgraceful, and we can't have the books looking like this."

Accordingly, Ruth Wynyard, the stationery monitress for the Third, requested Frieda to give her a packet of drawing-paper and a bottle of "Stickphast".

Frieda looked carefully at the list to make sure that Miss Stewart, the form mistress, had signed for this. Finding it in order, she produced the paper.

"An' the Stickphast too, please," said Ruth, a jolly, downright young person of about twelve.

"For that you must wait," said Frieda. "The Stickphast is on the top shelf, and I have not the ladder here."

"I'll go and get it!" And Ruth ran off to ask for the long ladder that was necessary for tackling the top shelves of the cupboard.

Frieda turned to Cornelia Flower of the Fourth,

discovered that those people required nothing more startling than three mapping-pens and a couple of exercise books for German, and gave her what she wanted. "And Miss Leslie says may we have blotchy too, please?" asked Cornelia.

"Why did you not write it down?" demanded Frieda suspiciously. "Form Four are most careless about this. You may have it this time; but another time you will have to go back and ask for a written note."

Cornelia assumed an injured look, but said nothing. Well she knew that the Fourth deserved suspicion. The form included some of the most mischievous girls in the school, herself among them, and it would not have been the first time they had tried to get stationery for their own nefarious purposes. On this occasion, however, Miss Leslie *had* sent the message, so she felt injured, and looked it.

Frieda doled it out – half a sheet for each girl, and a double sheet for the mistress. Then she dismissed Cornelia, and turned to Ruth, who had come back with the stepladder by this time, and was standing waiting.

"I will get down two or three pots while I am busy," said the prefect to the small girl, who had picked up her other stationery, and was waiting for the Stickphast. "Put down the other things, and take them as I hand them down, please."

Ruth dropped her stationery in the first place that came handy – the centre of the passage, and stood by to take the pots. Frieda mounted the ladder, and began to hand them down. There came the sound of running footsteps, and Margia Stevens came in sight, tearing for her life. She was late for her piano lesson, and Herr Anserl loathed being kept waiting two minutes. In her haste, she never noticed the pile of exercise books – Miss Wilson had demanded a fresh set of geography books for her form – and other oddments on the floor. She tripped over them, and fell, clutching at the nearest support – the stepladder. It swayed dangerously, and Frieda, with a wild yell, was precipitated on top of Ruth, a Stickphast bottle in each hand. The three went down together, and the Stickphast with them. One bottle crashed into the wall, smashing down on four others which Ruth had set on the floor. How they managed it no one ever knew; but every one of those four bottles broke, and when the three girls had struggled to their feet they were splashed with paste from head to foot. Ruth's hair was covered with a thick coating of paste; Margia's tunic was splashed from shoulder to knee, and her music had suffered badly; Frieda, being topmost, came off lightest, but even she was in a mess. The noise brought little Mademoiselle Lachenais from the Fifth, where she had been giving *dictée*, and her exclamations of horror added to the noise. Margia was the first to recover herself. Ruth had bumped her head against the wall, besides having Frieda fall on her. Frieda herself had caught her thumb against the ladder, and bent it right back, straining the muscles in doing so. Margia, beyond a graze or two, was uninjured, though that was more than could be said for her tunic. "Look at my music!" she wailed. "And Vater Bär is waiting for me!"

It was well for all concerned that Matron happened to be coming downstairs at the time and, hearing the noise, came to investigate. Her face when she beheld the white-wigged Ruth was a picture, as Paula von Rothenfels said when telling the story afterwards to Marie and Jo. By this time the entire Fifth was in the passage, all agog with excitement, and the clamour had caused other form-room doors to open. Matron took charge at once.

"Margia, are you hurt? Then go and change at once. Take your music to the kitchen as you go, and ask Luise if she can sponge it clean for you. – Ruth, you aren't killed, so stop crying like that. Twelve years old ought to be too big to be such a baby. – Frieda, have you hurt yourself? Then off you go to my room. – Mademoiselle, may one of your girls go and ask Moida to come and clear up this mess of paste? – And the rest of you, get back to your own rooms at once."

Matron was a martinet, so the girls did as they were told without any more ado, while she piloted the sobbing Ruth upstairs, where she bade her stop crying, and get her tunic and blouse off. "Your hair will have to be washed in any case," she said. – "Frieda, let me see your thumb."

She bathed the poor aching thumb and bound it up before she dismissed Frieda to change, and take her tunic and top down to the kitchen. Then she turned her attention to Ruth, whose bump showed itself in nothing more serious than a lump on the head. By the time the paste had been washed out of her hair, and she was in a fresh frock, this had resolved itself into a slight headache, and the only other signs of the accident were the wet boards, and an unsightly stain on the light green walls of the passage.

The school chuckled over it – all except Margia, who had had to face Herr Anserl's wrath, and Ruth, who was called to account for doing such a silly thing as to put a pile of exercise books in the middle of the floor.

"It's priceless!" laughed Jo. "Just what happened to Bernie, Frieda – d'you remember?"

Frieda nodded. "She spilt the red ink over herself and Grizel the first term of school."

"Remember Grizelda's face? Wasn't she mad?"

They laughed together, and the rest clamoured for an explanation. Jo gave it with many chuckles for the recollection of Mademoiselle's horror when she beheld Grizel and Bernhilda, as she thought, literally dripping with gore.

At *Mittagessen*, while they were still discussing the mishap of the morning, another occurred. Joey had a bad trick when she was talking of waving her hands about to illustrate her points. She had been lectured for it many times, and sundry minor accidents had been the results of this habit of hers. Today, as if the paste episode had not been enough, she must needs utilize her trick while relating some happening of the school's early days just at the moment that Luise set a dish of soup before her. Up went Jo's hand, and away went the soup, liberally bedewing Luise, the narratress herself, and little Peggy Burnett, who happened to be sitting at her right hand.

Peggy, more frightened than hurt, set up a roar like a miniature bull of Bashan, which drew the eyes of the whole room to them. Luise tossed up her hands in dismay, and dropped the dish which lay in fragments on the floor; while Jo, startled nearly out of her senses, sat in horrified silence.

This accident had been foretold not once, but many times. She stole a guilty look at Mademoiselle Lepâttre, who had risen at Peggy's yell, and now hastened to the rescue. Matron rushed up from the other side, and promptly sent Luise to the kitchen for more soup, while, at the same time, she lifted Peggy out of her chair and bore her off to be changed, dried, and comforted.

"But are you hurt, *ma petite*?" demanded Mademoiselle breathlessly of the actor of this little comedy.

The soup had been hot, and Jo had scalded one hand rather badly, but she was so much upset at the catastrophe itself that the Head had to repeat her question before she replied to it. "My hand stings a bit," she said stoically.

Mademoiselle drew the injured hand from its resting place on the girl's lap, and uttered horrified ejaculations at its condition. Miss Wilson came up from her seat, and took Jo off to have it properly dressed. Luise, having recovered herself, came back with fresh soup, and the little ones were served. Jo returned to the table with her hand bandaged, and was sent to sit with her compeers, while Marie took her place at what was known to the girls as "the babies' table".

Anyone would have thought that these two accidents would have satisfied the school for one day. But after *Kaffee und Kuchen*, when the Middles had strolled off to their own rooms to prepare for prep, some malignant imp prompted Elsie Carr and Maria Marani, sister of Gisela Mensch, and usually a quiet little person, to embark on a fierce argument as to whether it were possible to get one's head through the back of one of the peasant chairs which stood about the room when the desks were put up.

"Rats! It can't be done!" said Elsie scornfully.

"But it can!" maintained Maria, sticking to her point with unusual pertinacity for her.

"What? Get your head through that space? Talk sense, Maria!"

"I *am* talking sense!" retorted Maria.

"I tell you, you can't do it!"

"I will prove it to you!"

"So will I – so there!"

No need to say more. The pair got down on their knees behind two of the chairs and, by dint of pushing hard, both got their heads through the space.

"I said so!" crowed Maria triumphantly.

Evadne had come back from Innsbruck by this time, the tooth well and truly filled. She was full of spirits, having had a splendid time with the doctor once the business was over. Now she strolled round the pair, who resembled Chinese convicts more than anything else, and looked at them critically. "You've got them *through*, but I guess it won't be so easy to get them out," she remarked.

Alarmed at this suggestion, Elsie promptly tugged backwards and, as might have been expected, stuck.

Her example infected Maria, who did the same thing, with the same results. What was worse, even when they had calmed down, not all their own efforts nor the aid of their friends could release them from their weird position. It was left to Violet Allison to do the only sensible thing. She tore off to the prefects' room, whence she summoned the startled prefects, who came racing down, only to collapse on each other at the sight of the captive pair. Elsie had got to her feet, and was standing, holding the chair; but Maria was still on her knees struggling madly, while Cornelia Flower, Ilonka Barcocz, and Suzanne Mercier tugged at her in their efforts to free her.

Jo's heart had been heavy and her hand throbbing, but at the ridiculous spectacle she dropped into the nearest seat and sobbed with laughter. Frieda joined her, and Marie, Sophie, Simone, and Vanna followed their example.

"You mean pigs!" cried Elsie. "Can't you come and help us instead of giggling at us like a set of wild hyenas?"

"Say! I guess you folk are just too mean for words!" exclaimed Cornelia.

"I – I'm sorry!" choked Jo. "*Oh!* What a vision! Hold me up, someone!"

Frieda sat up, and looked at the pair. "We must try to push them first," she said seriously. "Jo, if you will pull Maria, I will push from the other side. We may be able to set them free that way."

Weeping with laughter, Jo got to her feet and staggered across to where Maria was still kneeling. Getting behind her, she waited till Frieda was ready to push from the other side, and between them they subjected the unhappy Maria to a species of torture that drew yells from her.

Sophie and Marie were no more successful with Elsie, and they finally gave it up.

"Why on earth the staff haven't been down on us before, I cannot think," said Vanna, who had been watching with interest.

"Over at Le Petit Chalet for a meeting," grunted Jo, who was breathless between her laughter and her efforts at freeing Maria.

"You'll have to saw through those chair-backs, I guess," said Evadne gloomily. "Say! Wouldn't it be awful if the saw was to slip just when you'd got through, and took a chunk out of their necks?"

This cheerful suggestion was met with further yells from the suffering Maria, and Jo promptly squashed the originator.

"Talk sense – if you *can*! – Margia, dash off to the kitchen, and ask Hansi for the saw from the woodshed. – Stop that awful yelling, Maria. You aren't killed yet, nor likely to be."

Margia raced off, and presently returned with the saw and Hansi, a stolid, fair-haired youth of about fifteen. Without more than a grunt he advanced to the first victim he saw – Elsie – and began to saw evenly through the back of the chair. The girls held their breath while he was busy. They were not certain that the saw might not slip as Evadne had suggested. However, he knew his work too well for that. Ten minutes' hard work freed the pair, and then Jo dismissed him with a word of thanks, and sent Sophie to ring the bell for prep.

"As for you two, I mean to find out what you were doing to get in such a mess," she announced. "Go and make yourselves fit to be seen, and then come to the prefects' room. The rest of you, get your books out and begin. Prep is twenty minutes late as it is."

Leaving Simone, who was in charge this evening, to see that she was obeyed, she turned on her heel and marched out of the room, followed by the rest of her compeers. The scared Middles, sufficiently subdued by what had happened, settled down to their work more quickly than might have been expected, and when the staff returned to the school an hour later, they found everything more or less normal, save for the fact that two of the chairs in the Middles' common room had had their backs sawed in half.

Meanwhile, the prefects had got to the bottom of the affair, and told the guilty pair exactly what they thought of them.

"You might be a couple of babies," Joey had wound up. "You ought both to be ashamed of yourselves. As it is, the school property is damaged because you choose to behave like idiots. Well, you can both call Saturday off – and think yourselves lucky you're escaping so lightly," she added.

Then she sent them to their work and addressed herself to her own. Elsie and Maria, both deprived of the weekend trip to the Sonnalpe, returned to prep sadder and wiser girls. As for the staff, when they had heard the prefects' report they looked at each other helplessly. "Whatever next?" demanded Miss Annersley.

There was no reply.

CHAPTER IX

Better News

SOMEHOW THE WEEK DRAGGED ALONG to the end. After the last exhibition, the Middles curbed themselves somewhat. No one wanted to lose the trip up to the

Sonnalpe, so Jo's swift retribution for the necessary destruction of the chair-backs acted as a deterrent on whatever wild schemes might have floated through the brains of the more irresponsible members of the Third and Fourth forms. Jo herself tried to bury her fears in hard work, and threw herself into prep and games with all the intentness of which she was capable. Her example infected the rest of the Sixth, and the staff had an easy week of it, so far as work was concerned. Only Frieda, besides Marie, knew what black dread lay at the bottom of the head girl's heart and overshadowed her days. The three never talked of it, once the young Innsbrucker had been told, but it was continually in their minds, and they were very quiet.

Friday night came, and brought with it the first boating of the season. It was still much too cold for swimming, early May though it was. But for a week the weather had been calm, and on this evening the lake lay like glass beneath a soft blue sky, where a few fleecy clouds floated like a tiny galleons.

Miss Wilson came into the common room after *Kaffee*, calling, "Hurry and change into boating-kit, girls! It is such a fine evening, we are all going on the lake."

The girls fled at top speed. Really, prep should have come in about twenty minutes' time, so they were thrilled at the thought of missing it. As for "Bill", she returned to her colleagues laughing. "Great excitement!" she said.

"That was to be expected, wasn't it?" asked pretty Miss Stewart, who was known as "Charlie" among the girls, Jo having first christened her "Bonny Prince Charlie" on seeing that her initials were C. E. As a matter of fact, Miss Stewart's names were Constance Elizabeth, but the girls did not know that, and the name held.

Miss Wilson turned to her now with a smile. "Even Jo cheered up," she said.

The staff looked grave. They of course knew the news about the Robin, and they had been very lenient with Jo this week, excusing any shortcomings in the way of concentration in a manner that ought to have startled her if she had been in a condition to realize it.

Miss Annersley now got to her feet, and went to the window. "I wish they would send down some news," she said restlessly. "It is nearly a week since that man from Vienna came. Surely he must have found out by this time!"

"He may want to keep the child under observation for a time before giving his verdict," said Miss Leslie, the maths mistress.

"Oh, I know." Miss Annersley made an impatient gesture. "They will let us know as soon as possible. But this waiting is trying for anyone. What it must be like to Jo, I shudder to think."

"I rather wonder at Madame telling Jo," remarked Miss Nalder, the gym mistress. "Surely it is unkind to have left her to fret all this week about the Robin?"

Miss Annersley shook her head. "Jo would never have forgiven them if they had left her in ignorance of anything so vital. Besides, they have always taken her into their councils. I believe they even discussed coming here with her before they decided anything; and she was little more than a baby then."

"I see," Miss Nalder got up from her chair, and picked up her cap from the table where it lay. "Well, I must be going. The girls will be ready in a minute. Bill, you are coming ? – And Charlie? – What about you, Nan?"

"In about half an hour," said Miss Annersley. "I must get some of the arrears of correcting wiped off first."

The younger mistresses strolled out, laughing and talking, and Miss Annersley, left to herself, ran down to the study and sat down at the telephone. Two minutes later she had got on to Die Rosen, and was demanding Madge.

"Mrs Russell speaking," came back to her. "Who is it – oh, Hilda! Is anything wrong with the school?"

"Nothing," said Miss Annersley. "They are going boating just now, as the evening is so calm. I am supposed to be working off some correcting, but I wanted to talk to you, so it must wait."

"What is the trouble?" demanded Madge.

"Just the trouble we heard of at the weekend. Is there anything definite yet?"

"Yes. Quite definite news now."

"Oh – is it good?" There was an eagerness in Miss Annersley's voice that was proof of the dearness of the Robin to everyone.

Over the phone came the sound of Madge Russell's soft laugh as she replied, "Better than we had hoped for. But I can't tell you anything more till Jo hears. It wouldn't be fair to her. But we've had an awful week of it. The Robin has been tried and tested in every possible way, which has made her very cross and fractious, because we couldn't keep her from knowing about a good deal of it. However, you'll hear all in good time."

"Aggravating creature!" laughed Miss Annersley. "Well, the girls will be up on Saturday as usual, so I suppose we shall get all news when they come down."

"Yes. You *do* understand, don't you, Hilda? Jo must know first – it's her right. She adores the Robin. Tell her, if you like, what I have told you. It will relieve her mind. I was going to ring her up this evening, in any case."

"Thank you. Yes; I should like to tell her. I only hope it doesn't upset her to the point of making her play any mad tricks. We've had enough of *them* for the time being!"

"My dear! What *do* you mean? This sounds most intriguing."

"Jo can tell you when she comes," laughed Miss Annersley. "I must run now, or they will think I am never coming." She rang off, and then went out to the lake, where the girls were enjoying the sensation of being on the water once more. A chorus of shouts hailed her advent, and she was invited into three separate boats. She elected to join Joey's, and when they finally came in she invited the head girl to walk back to the school with her. "Can you leave the others for a while, Joey? I should like a word with you."

"Oh, my stars!" thought Jo. "What have I done *now*?"

Miss Annersley, watching her expressive face, smiled to herself, for she knew what the girl was thinking. "It's some news I have for you, Jo," she said.

"News?" Jo looked at her.

"Yes; rather nice news too, I think."

"Are St Scholastika's to have boats, after all?" ventured Jo.

St Scholastika's was the other school, at the opposite side of the lake. Once upon a time there had been a deadly feud between its members and those of the Chalet School. That was all at an end, however, and now the two schools were good friends. Miss Browne, the Head of the Saints, as the girls called them, had a nervous dread of the water, and had so far refused to allow her girls to have boating. The Chaletians, however, lived in hopes that she would yield shortly. Then they planned to have races, and a regatta even. So Jo, fresh from an hour's boating, naturally thought of this.

Miss Annersley shook her head as she drew the girl apart and they strolled along the shore. "No, Jo; it isn't anything to do with school."

"*Not* school? What – Miss Annersley! Do you – is it – the Robin?"

Miss Annersley nodded. "I rang up the Sonnalpe before I came out to you. There is better news, Jo, and your sister said I might tell you."

"The Robin is all right, then?" Jo's face was white and tense with emotion, and her eyes looked unnaturally large.

Miss Annersley slipped an arm through hers. "Not quite that, Joey. Madame would tell me nothing definite. She said it was your right to know first, and you would hear when you went up tomorrow. But it is better than they had hoped. Why, Joey!"

For Joey had turned away with a sob. The mistress pulled her in at the gate, and to a little arbour which was screened with climbing roses. Here she made her sit down, and Jo wept away the bitter grieving that had been welling up in her heart all the week. Miss Annersley left her to herself for a time, standing in the doorway to screen her from any passers-by. Presently, as she stood watching the sky, she felt a touch on her arm, and turning round saw Joey, with red eyes and tearstained face, but with all the strain gone out of it. "Miss Annersley, you are a *ripper*! Sorry I made such an ass of myself, but – but—"

"It has been a hard week for you, Jo," said Miss Annersley. "You have been very plucky over it, I think. I knew you needed that, and you will be better for it. Now, the gong has been rung some time, and we are both late for *Abendessen*. Come upstairs to my snuggery, and I will ask Luise to let us have something there. Then I think you'd better go to bed. I expect your head is aching."

"It is, rather," said Jo.

"I thought so. Come along. You needn't see anyone tonight."

"I think I should like to tell Frieda and Marie. They knew."

"Very well. I will tell them to come to you after you have gone to bed, and the rest shall leave you alone. Now, come and see what we can coax out of Luise."

She led the way to the tiny sitting room that was hers

by right of being senior mistress, and presently Luise, the chief maid at the school, appeared with basins of delicious soup, and crisp little rolls. These were followed by fruit and custard, and then Miss Annersley made tea with her electric kettle, and this refreshed Jo more than anything. Tea was in the nature of a treat at the Chalet, where the usual drink was coffee made very milky. When the meal was over, Miss Annersley sent the head girl off to bed, and after cautioning the rest against disturbing her, caught Frieda and Marie, and sent them to her. Jo told her news with a happy face, and the other two rejoiced with her. "Don't let Simone know you've been here, if you can help it," she warned them, as they left her to try to finish their prep. "I don't want any scenes."

They agreed. Simone Lecoutier was, unfortunately, inclined to be very jealous. There had been scenes in the past, when Simone had made herself thoroughly miserable because Jo insisted on being friends with other girls, and though she had improved, and learnt self-control since then, she was still very tenacious of her rights as Jo's closest friend.

Duly warned, the other two slipped away to the prefects' room, and were thankful to find that Simone was downstairs with some of the others. They settled down to their prep, and were soon so busy that when she came in she decided against disturbing them. So the dreaded scene was avoided, and there was peace that night. The next morning, Dr Mensch came at eight o'clock for those who were to spend the weekend at the Sonnalpe. His reason for this was that the days were growing hot now, and if it were left much later, it meant that the girls had the long, arduous climb in the heat of the day.

Joey raced to meet him, but beyond telling her that things were better than they had hoped at the Sonnalpe, he refused to enlighten her at all, and she had to possess her soul in patience till they reached Die Rosen, where Madge stood at the door, with the Robin at her side and David in her arms. Stacie was lying in her chair on the veranda, and Peggy and Rix were rolling on the grass. Joey kissed the tinies, and held the Robin closely to her. Then she turned to her sister. Madge was smiling wholeheartedly at her, and her eyes were wells of happiness once more.

"It is well?" asked Jo, using Italian so that none but her sister might understand her.

Madge nodded. "It is very well, Joey." Then she set her son down on the big rug on the grass, and sent the Robin for Rosa, his little nurse.

Jo watched the child go. "It – it—"

"No, Joey. There is nothing to fear there. The lungs are quite sound, and she is getting stronger. The other symptoms were from her rapid growth. Of course she needs the greatest care still. Herr Schiedmann says that she must stay up here till the growing years are past. But he thinks that, given ordinary circumstances, all fear of the horrid thing is past. But the Robin will not come back to the Chalet School, Jo. She will be here for the next ten years, probably, unless we take her to other similar places. So – and this is a piece of news I want you to keep to yourself for the rest of the term – we are talking of opening an annexe of the Chalet School up here for delicate children like the Robin and Amy Stevens. And who do you think is coming out to take charge?"

Jo looked at her eagerly. "Who? Oh, Madge! Not Juliet?"

Madge nodded. "Yes; Juliet will be Head; and to help her we are to have Grizel and Gertrud. Some of the frailer members of the school will be moved up here next term, and they are going to build an electric railway up the mountainside, so that some of the rest of the staff can come up, say, twice a week for lessons."

"Whatever next!" cried Jo, as Rosa came for Baby David, and the Robin grabbed her hand. "*Aren't* we coming on!"

CHAPTER X

Sunday

WHAT A WEEKEND THAT WAS!

In her joy, Jo, as usual, went to the other extreme, and became the imp she had been less than two years ago. Forgotten her obligations as head girl! Forgotten all her good resolutions! She led the family at Die Rosen a dance that weekend with her pranks, and infuriated Stacie to the point of declaring that she wished Joey had not come up that week.

Frieda was there, but she had naturally gone to her brother's. The other two were Violet Allison and Peggy Burnett. Violet was there on Eustacia's account, and Peggy had been one of the Robin's greatest chums. The two little ones were kept to the nursery very much, for Jo's wild spirits might have proved tiring for the Robin, though she generally managed to control herself when the child was about. But the others had to put up with her nonsense, though Frieda did get a respite when she was at Das Pferd.

"Jo! For goodness' sake get a book and sit down somewhere!" cried Madge in exasperated tones on the Sunday afternoon, when finally even she was tired out. "If you go on like this, you'll end by crying."

Jo grimaced at her. "I look like it, don't I?"

"You'll have a dose of salts and senna, young woman," warned Dr Jem from the deck-chair where he was taking his ease.

"Don't be a pig, Jem! Oh! I can hear David crying!"

Joey dashed off in the direction of the little lawn where her nephew was supposed to be having his afternoon nap in his pram. Rosa, sister of Marie who ruled the kitchen department of Die Rosen with a hand of iron, had walked up that morning to see her sister, and she was pushing his pram backwards and forwards, trying to soothe him. But David was upset for some reason or other, and he refused to be quieted. He howled lustily, and not even when his young aunt, with a complete disregard for rules, lifted him up and cuddled him against her, did he stop. Madge came to see what was wrong, but could make nothing of him. Finally, they took him to the house, where he was undressed, and examined for pins and other discomforts. There was nothing there. He was quite well, too, so far as they could gather. The doctor, summoned to his son, confirmed this, and advised them to put him back in his pram, and leave him.

This Spartan advice Madge took, but David wailed on, till she felt desperate. "There *must* be something wrong with him!" she exclaimed at length. "It's no use, Jem! I'm going to take him up. It isn't like him to cry like this; and he may hurt himself if he's allowed to continue."

"It's your fault, Jo," said the doctor, when his wife had gone to pick up her son. "You're a disturbing element today, and David feels it."

"Rats!" said Joey derisively.

"No; it is true. You'd better calm down a little, I think, before you upset the rest of the household. Come, Joey; it isn't like you to get excited to this pitch."

"I'm so glad about the Robin," said Jo wistfully.

He ran his slender surgeon's hand over her wild mop.

"I know. But you must try to take it more quietly. Apart from anything else, you'll make yourself ill if you get worked up like this. Now go and lie down like a good kid till *Kaffee*, and give Madge a chance to calm Davy down."

Jo went off. Truth to tell, she was feeling worn out by this time, and in need of a rest.

The entire household breathed more quietly after the doctor slipped upstairs, and returned to report that she was fast asleep. "She needs it," he said gravely to his wife, when they were alone. "I doubt if she slept much last night; and we must remember what a severe illness she had last autumn. In some ways, I have been wondering if it wouldn't be as well to have her up here when you open the annexe."

Madge turned eyes of horror on him. "Jem! Jo isn't ill?"

"No, no!" he replied quickly. "She really is much stronger than I ever thought possible. But she does such mad things, and she feels so intensely. She has lost weight this past week with worry over the Robin. A nature like hers is sometimes more of a curse than a blessing. She has wonderful moments of happiness, I know. But her sufferings more than pay for them."

"That is why she can write," replied Madge, as she cuddled a now pacified and sleeping David to her. "All creative artists are the same. It is part of the gift, Jem."

He nodded. "I know that. But I wish we could help Joey to control herself better. I am afraid she may suffer so terribly some day."

Madge looked troubled. "I hope not. Perhaps this year of responsibility may help her. In any case, Jem, unless her health makes it imperative, I think she is better at Briesau. For one thing, it is further from the sanatorium and all that sort of thing, which I don't think too good for her – not as a general rule, at any rate."

"There, I agree," said the doctor, as he filled his pipe. "Jo is too impressionable altogether."

"Well, then?"

"Oh, you are quite right. Jo must stay where she is. Also, she must try to control herself *of* herself. After all, we can't take all, or even much of the burden off her. She'll worry through all right, I expect. There's any amount of good stuff in Joey."

They turned to other subjects after that, and chatted quietly till *Kaffee* came, and with it the girls. Jo looked better for her nap. There was a faint colour in her face, and her eyes were not so heavy. Violet and Stacie, who had read quietly, were eager for talk, and before long, Jo was convulsing the rest with her account of the week's happenings.

"You awful people!" exclaimed Madge, wiping the tears of laughter from her eyes after she had heard her sister's graphic description of the predicament of Elsie and Maria. "Whatever will you do next?"

"I like that!" Jo sounded injured. "I hadn't a thing to do with it!"

"But are the pretty chairs hurt?" the Robin wanted to know.

"The backs are sawn in half," replied Jo. "Hansi had to take a piece out of Maria's, because of her hair – she has such quantities. Oh, Madge! If you had only seen them! I nearly made myself sick with laughing!"

"I don't wonder," chuckled the doctor. "Well, it's a pity about the chairs; but I suppose you couldn't have let them go about with chairs round their necks for the rest of their lives."

"Herr Schneider, the carpenter-man, is going to mend them," said Violet, "and Elsie and Maria have to pay out of their pocket money – Mademoiselle said so."

"Quite right, too," said Madge, suddenly remembering that she was a headmistress, in name, at any rate.

"I *wish* I had seen it!"

Jo turned to Stacie, who had breathed this wistful remark, and chuckled. "I wish you had. Never mind; you ought to be getting down again next term, and they certainly won't stop their monkey tricks because of that one accident."

She caught her sister's eye at this point, and, remembering what Madge had told her when they had first come up, she gasped.

"What an idiot I am!" she thought to herself. "Of course Stacie will stay up here if they open that annexe affair. It would only be common sense. I wonder if she knows anything about it?"

"Coo-ee!" came a call at that moment; and then Frieda came running up the garden path to them, to say that Gottfried was going to walk over to see a patient at the other end of the alm, and would take them if they cared to go.

"Rather!" cried Jo, who had only been there once or twice before.

"Who's going?"

"Me, please," said Violet. "I've never been there."

"Peggy, do you want to come?"

Peggy Burnett, a peaceful little person of nearly ten, shook her head. "No thank you, Joey, I'd rather stay with Robin, and play with her new puzzle."

"But you promised to put me to bed, Joey," protested the last-named small girl.

"So I did. But I'll be back long before you go to bed, darling," said Joey. "Gottfried won't want to stay long, will he, Frieda?"

Frieda shook her head. "No; because it would leave Gisela too long alone. He said we should go there and come straight back. We shall have returned by half-past four."

"Good! Then we can do it. What time do you go to bed, *Bübchen*?"

"Seven on Sundays," said the Robin, her lovely little face clearing.

"Then that's all right. – Righto, Frieda; we'll come – Violet and me."

"What English for the head girl!" laughed Madge. "Trot along, then. I don't suppose Gottfried wants to be kept waiting. – Is he ready, Frieda?"

"Yes, Madame. He said he would wait for us at home, as it was on the way."

"Then off you trot. Tell Gisela I'll be along later. I want to see her about those new frocks for Baby Natalie."

Frieda nodded, and Jo and Violet galloped off to seek their hats and coats, for, warm as it was in the sheltered garden, it would be chilly along the alm. They all set off, taking Rufus with them. The big dog was always given exercise, but to have his much-loved mistress take him made him feel that this walk was a very special one. He missed Jo when she was down at the school, and now she was here again, and not unhappy as she had been on her last visit, but her old cheery self. Once more Rufus, who could sense her every mood, raced up and down, more like a puppy than a grown-up dog.

The girls came back at half-past six glowing and merry, for Dr Gottfried had made them walk at a brisk pace. Joey went off to fulfil her promise to the Robin, and Frieda followed to give a hand with Peggy and Rix, who were wildly excited because they had been allowed to stay up an hour later than usual in honour of Auntie Jo's visit, and were more than Marie could cope with by herself. When the four babies – David was already asleep in his cot – were safely off, the elder girls came downstairs, and sat in the big salon, talking quietly.

Towards the end of the evening, just as Gottfried came to take his young sister back to Das Pferd, Joey spoke about the Robin. "I am more thankful than I can say," she said. "It's been a nightmare this past week. I couldn't give my mind to anything."

Only she, Frieda, and Stacie were there, Violet having gone upstairs ten minutes before. Stacie looked up at her, colour flushing her normally pale face. "It has been bad for you, Jo," she said. "But I think I have suffered quite as much. If anything – had – gone wrong, I should always have felt that it was my fault, you see."

Jo got up from her chair and went across the room to her. "Never say that again," she said gently. "Jem told me that though it might have hastened things a little, yet if it had come to the worst, it could only have meant that – nothing could have been done, *nothing*."

Then Gottfried and the Russells appeared, and Frieda had to go home. But Stacie never forgot that, and she always felt a deep gratitude to Jo for saying it.

CHAPTER XI

Half-Term Rejoicings

THE TERM SPED FAST AFTER that. Work and games went on as usual. Early in June, the Chalet School played St Scholastika's at cricket, and beat them by seventy-nine runs. Tennis matches between the forms took place, and the Fifth carried all before them. In Louise Redfield and Margia Stevens they had a formidable pair of champions, while Signa Johansen and Giovanna Donati made a good second-string pair. In the Sixth, Frieda Mensch paired with Carla von Flügen for first couple, and Simone Lecoutier and Lis Bernaldi were second couple.

Jo, who was excellent at cricket, was too erratic to do much at tennis. On her day she was brilliant, her service being almost untakeable. But then, as Miss Nalder said with a sigh, her day came so rarely. Marie von Eschenau was also better at cricket, rather to the surprise of everyone. Marie's loveliness and her slight frame gave no clue to the wonderful force of her drives, and she was a natural slow bowler, with a nasty off-break that finished the St Scholastika batting.

Then, one evening when they were strolling down to the lake, Joey calmly remarked, "Well, by this time next week we shall be packing for Oberammergau, I suppose."

"It is, then, so near?" cried Simone, who was at her side as usual.

"Next week as ever is. Won't it be gorgeous? Juliet will be here too. She finishes tomorrow, and is coming out at once. Grizel will be up on Saturday. If only Gisela, Wanda, and Bernhilda could come, it would be like old times!" sighed conservative Jo.

Marie laughed. "Gisela could hardly bring Baby Natalie; and Wanda's little Kurt is only three weeks old tomorrow."

"Awful!" declared Jo. "Gisela and Wanda proud mammas! I suppose Bernie will be the next. Oh dear! We shall all be grannies before we know where we are!"

The others burst into peals of laughter, and Simone murmured something about, "Not before I have my *bachot*, I hope."

"Yes; that's the next thing," wailed the pessimist. "*You* will go and be a learned lady. Juliet will have her BSc and be – er—"

"Be what?" demanded Margia, who was with them.

"Nothing."

"Rats to that! Go on, Jo! You began to say something all right!"

"Isn't it a lovely evening?" queried naughty Jo.

"Joey! Don't be a pig! Tell us what you were going to say!"

"Never you mind. I can't tell you, anyhow. You'll hear sooner or later."

A howl of indignation arose at this. "Jo! You—"

"Hush – hush!" said Jo reprovingly. "Little girls shouldn't call names."

"Well, what is Juliet going to be?"

"A maths mistress," replied Joey, suddenly remembering that at any rate *this* was no secret. And with this the rest had to be satisfied. "How awful!" thought Jo to herself, as she finally made her escape. "I very nearly let the cat out of the bag. I *must* be more careful!" Luckily, everyone was too much excited at the near prospect of half term and Oberammergau to remember much about it, though Frieda, Marie, and Simone had fits of wondering. They knew better than to attack Jo on the subject, however.

"All the same, I wonder what she meant," said Marie to Frieda in private, "for you know that nonsense about maths mistresses was just one way out of a difficulty. Jo knows something that will happen, and Juliet is to be in it."

Further than that they could not go, and as Peggy Burnett came out in spots the next day, they were all too occupied in dreading measles to think about it again.

David's birthday, which had occurred the previous month, had been celebrated by the entire school's joining in getting a magnificent set of Hornby railway engine and lines and carriages for him. As Jo had pointed out when it had been discussed, it was rather soon for it, but it could be kept for him till he had grown to it. In the meantime he was quite happy with balls and furry animals, which the girls knitted with wool. Two days before half term began, Mrs Russell made her appearance with him, and announced that they had come to see the girls off to Oberammergau, and would stay at the school while the pupils and staff were absent.

He had grown into a regular boy now, with solemn dark eyes, his mother's curly crop, and his father's firm mouth and chin. In his little rompers he spent most of the day in the flower-garden, only coming in at bedtime, and his mother resigned herself to seeing next to nothing of him, for the girls quarrelled as to who should look after him, and put him to bed, and dress him in the mornings. During school hours, it is true, Mrs Russell might have had him to herself; but she yielded to the entreaties of the girls, and resumed her old classes, while her son spent his time with the mistress thus unexpectedly free from duty.

Finally, the Thursday evening came, and after *Kaffee* the girls scattered to their dormitories to pack for the trip. One case between two girls was to be allowed, and they were to take as little as possible. Juliet, who had arrived that morning, took the opportunity to have a chat with her old Head, and tell her all the news. The younger girls, many of whom had not known her before, looked at her with awe, for Jo had told them a good deal about her. She was tall and very slim, with a mass of fair hair – which she wore in a coronal of plaits round her head – and dark eyes. She was dainty in her dress, and when she came among them like one of themselves they all became her instant slaves.

Grizel Cochrane had left much more recently, and she consequently aroused less interest, but she was welcomed very vociferously none the less.

"Glad to be back, old thing?" asked Joey of Juliet when the greetings were over.

"Very glad," replied Juliet emphatically. "And it's for good now."

"Fancy you a BSc!" went on the irreverent one. "What is the world coming to?"

Juliet laughed. "I wonder! Come along and have a chat. It's ages since we saw each other – not since January."

"Well, much hasn't happened since then," returned Jo, with a lack of English construction shocking in a future novelist.

"Never mind. I want to hear all about everything, so come along."

Grizel was busy with Marie, Frieda, and Simone, and the rest of the party were variously occupied, so Jo went off, and she and Juliet discussed the new departure in all its aspects, once the news of the term had been given.

"And we set off for Oberammergau tomorrow!" sighed the head girl rapturously, when the other subject had been dealt with. "One of the dreams of my life come true!"

"And one of mine, too," said Juliet. "Jo," she went on, with a change of subject, "have you heard from Bernhilda lately?"

"I haven't, but Frieda has," said Jo, staring at her. "Why?"

"Because she has written to me to say that she and Kurt are coming north for little Kurt's christening. I only heard the day I came out here. As a matter of fact—"

Juliet's voice suddenly trailed off, and Jo, looking at her in surprise, was amazed to see that she was unusually flushed for her.

"What on earth—" she began. Then she stopped.

They had been walking by the lake, and had been gradually nearing the Kron Prinz Karl, the big hotel that dominated the little peninsula of Briesau. On the low-railed, wooden veranda the few visitors who had already come out were sitting reading and chatting. Among them were the Hillises, and with them was a young man who Jo had not seen before. It was at this group that Juliet was looking with that colour in her face and a new look in her eyes. Jo groaned inwardly, for she had never seen Juliet like this.

"We're all getting far too grown-up!" she thought. Then, because she was a good sport, she said aloud, "Hello! There are the Hillises! You don't know them. Come along, and I'll introduce you."

She led the way to the veranda, followed by a silent Juliet. But she was totally unprepared for what happened. Little Mrs Frank Hillis looked up as the two girls approached, and opened her lips to welcome Jo, whom she knew very well. Then her gaze fell on Juliet, and her eyes took on a look of surprise that changed to a hardness that amazed Jo.

"Good afternoon, Mrs Hillis," she cried. "Here's my friend, Miss Carrick, who has just come from England. She's one of our old girls, and has been at the Royal Holloway College. Now she's got her BSc, and she's come back to us to teach in the school."

Here she stopped, for she could feel the chill in the air, however hard she tried to ignore it. Mrs Hillis was flushed, and her eyes looked stormy, while Juliet was as white as a sheet, and looked distressed. Mr Hillis, who saw nothing but a tall, striking-looking girl with his old friend's sister-in-law, and had not noticed his wife's expression, held out a hand, and proceeded to introduce the other man.

"Hello, Joey! This is my wife's brother, Donal O'Hara, just come from Ireland to spend his vac with us. Only, as there's no room where we are, he's parking himself here."

Joey shook hands with the stranger, and then glanced at Juliet. That young lady kept hers stiffly at her side, and merely bent a haughty head in acknowledgment of the introduction. "Mr O'Hara and I have met before," she said. "Mrs Hillis was in her fourth year at college when I was in my first."

The ice in her voice made impressionable Jo shiver.

Mr Hillis suddenly seemed to realize that all was not well, and opened his mouth in surprise. It was left to Juliet to end the position. "I think we must go now, Jo," she said. "Madame is sure to be wanting us; and you still have some things to do, haven't you, before *Abendessen*?"

After this broad hint there was nothing for it but to acquiesce, and Jo agreed that she was busy. The two girls made their farewells, and left, and the visitors remained where they were. On the way back, Joey stole a look at her friend. Juliet's face was stormy, and her eyes were hard in a way that the younger girl had never seen them. She would have liked to ask questions; but with Juliet looking like that she knew it would be no use, so she refrained, and they returned to the school in silence.

For the rest of the evening Juliet fought shy of Jo, and was extremely occupied with the others, so that the head girl had to go off to bed at nine with her curiosity unsatisfied. But she vowed to herself that she would get to the bottom of things before she was many days older, or her name was not Josephine Bettany.

CHAPTER XII

Juliet's Secret

IT WAS NOT TILL THEY were on the train for Oberammergau, and were speeding away from Innsbruck that Joey got her chance with Juliet. That young lady had avoided her most conspicuously since the previous evening, and it is certain that, had she known of the head girl's manoeuvres, she would have insisted on joining some of the others. As it was, she climbed into the carriage, and took her seat on the little platform on a case without any suspicion of what was to follow. Joey mounted after her; made signs to the faithful Simone, who would have joined them, to go away, and settled down beside her friend. Simone was desperately jealous of Juliet, but she knew better than to force herself on the pair in face of Joey's emphatic gestures, so she heaved a sigh and joined Frieda and Marie at the other end of the platform. They had noticed Jo's action and, full of sympathy for her, since they had guessed that something was wrong, swung their case round, so that their backs were to the other two, and Simone had, perforce, to resign herself to the inevitable. It is to be doubted, however, if she got much good of the wonderful scenery through which they passed, and which enchanted the others. She was too much occupied in wondering what it was Jo and Juliet were discussing so earnestly.

Meanwhile Juliet, having discovered what her friend had done, looked round for some means of deliverance. Short of getting up and joining another group there was nothing she could do. Owing to the play, the train was packed, and there was no room anywhere else. In any case, this must come sooner or later, and she preferred, on the whole, to get it over. So she moved up to give Jo more room, and said as cordially as she could, "Come along! Heaps of room here!"

Jo sat down, and there was silence for a moment. Then the younger girl drew closer to her friend.

Juliet looked at her with a half-smile. "What is it, baby?"

"How did you get to know Mrs Frank and her brother?"

Juliet's eyes darkened, and her lips set in a firm line. "It's not an easy story, Jo."

"Can't you tell me, then? I won't bother if you'd rather not; but we're almost like sisters, and things that affect you mean a lot to me." Jo's eyes were wistful as she said it.

Juliet slipped a hand round the slim brown paw lying in her lap. "I know that, Joey. Well, I never meant to tell anyone; but you *are* a different story, after all, aren't you? But I told you last night that Kay O'Hara was in her fourth year at Holloway when I was in my first."

"That didn't tell me much."

"No; perhaps not. Well, she was. Of course, the fourth-year people are a very gorgeous lot, as a rule, and don't have much to do with freshers. But Kay seemed to take a fancy to me. She was wonderfully sweet and kind. I – liked her awfully." Juliet's lips quivered, and Jo looked at her sharply.

"But she wasn't kind afterwards?"

"You'd better hear the whole story, and then you can judge."

Jo turned, so that she gazed out at the wooded slopes up which the train was speeding, and when the soft, black eyes were turned from her, Juliet spoke; slowly at first, but later with more fluency. "Kay was good to me. I was dreadfully homesick for Briesau and all you people. Remember, it was the first real *home* I'd ever had. *You* know how my own people regarded me – as an incubus, of whom they were only too thankful to be well rid. Then Madame came, with her heavenly kindness, and there were you and the Robin – in a lesser sense, Grizel. I had two years of that, and it was new to me. Can you imagine how I felt when I went to England, and found myself alone for the first time after two years of love and fellowship, and – *wanting*?"

Jo nodded. "I can guess," she murmured.

"You know, Joey," Juliet went on slowly, "it was the first time in my life that I had ever been wanted by anyone. To leave my home and go right away, all those thousands of miles, meant a fairly big wrench for me."

"It must have been awful," agreed Jo.

"Well, you can guess what Kay's kindness was, then?"

"Of course. It must have been like seeing your guardian angel suddenly when you had been afraid in the dark."

"Something like that. I'm not of the worshipping kind, but I just worshipped Kay O'Hara."

Juliet paused, her face twisted with distress. Jo's fingers closed on hers, and there was silence for the moment. Presently, Juliet released her hand, and smiled at her friend. "Thanks, Joey. How you understand, kid!"

"I love you," said Jo softly. "Love brings understanding."

Juliet nodded. "Perhaps so. I don't know – I haven't found it always so. Well; there's no sense in dragging this out. To shorten things a bit, I met Kay's brother, Donal. You saw him at the Kron Prinz Karl yesterday. We liked each other. At first Kay seemed awfully pleased. She was engaged herself, to Frank Hillis; and she seemed very fond of me. Then, suddenly, her manner changed. She turned quite cold, and would have nothing to do with me. I couldn't understand it at first. I couldn't think of anything I'd done. I found out later, when she had ended all our friendship as far as she could. Someone, whose people had been in India, had recognized me, and knew about me, and told her about me – my people, and so on."

Jo was dumb with sympathy. She could think of nothing to say. Her eyes filled with tears, but she made no movement.

Juliet knew what was happening, and went on quietly.

"Kay is very proud. The O'Haras are a very old family, and they are very proud of their ancient lineage, and – and the fact that – that all their men have been upright and honourable. Your brother Dick told Madame that my father had made India too hot to hold him. It was true, and it was this that Gertrude Emery had told Kay, and Kay was furious to think that the daughter of such a man should have come so near to entering their family. She refused even to speak to me, and she told Donal all sorts of things about my father. He is her twin, you know, and she has always had a great deal of influence over him. What she may have told him, I don't know. But, anyhow, he left off writing to me, and never came to see me. At first I tried to think I didn't care, but I always knew I did. That was why I was so ill last summer. Now you know the story. Perhaps I oughtn't to have told you, but you aren't a baby now, Jo – and you are one of the few people who really *care*!"

Jo nodded again. She was gazing out over the summer landscape as it flashed past.

Juliet spoke again. "I haven't told Madame, Joey. Leave me to do that, darling."

Again the younger girl nodded. "Of course. And, Juliet—"

Juliet turned and looked her full in the face. "Yes?"

"It – it doesn't hurt so much *now*, does it?"

"Joey, it always hurts. But you can get accustomed to anything in time, so I suppose it will get better some day. Don't think any more about it, Joey, *Herzliebchen*."

Jo gave a little smile. "I'll do better than that."

A sudden horror of what Jo *might* do seized Juliet. She caught the younger girl by the shoulder. "Jo! You are not to interfere!"

"I won't. I've got more sense than that. But I *can* pray that things may come right, and I will. I believe – we both do – that God will answer all prayers if they are only made, believing that He really hears and helps us. I can feel what it has all meant to you, Juliet, and I know He will help us. So I'm going to ask Him to put things straight for you and – what did you say his name was – Donald?"

"Donal," corrected Juliet. "It is the Irish form, I believe. He was called after the great O'Hara who ruled the tribe in the days of the Tudors some time. It is a favourite name of theirs."

"Very well. I will pray that you and Donal may somehow put things straight."

Juliet was silenced. It was very rarely that Jo spoke of her faith. Such things lay very deeply with her, and she found it difficult to express them. But she had worked out her own creed, and her faith in God's ultimate goodness was unshakable.

Ten minutes later, the train ran into the little station of Oberammergau, and they were all busily occupied in sorting out their baggage and going off to the various houses that were to accommodate them for the short time of their stay.

CHAPTER XIII

Oberammergau

OBERAMMERGAU IS SO WELL KNOWN that it needs little description. The village lies, embosomed by mountains which in the spring and summer are green with forests that clothe the slopes. To the end of the village lies the theatre, open to the sky, with its huge auditorium forming a horseshoe all round the stage. The village itself is typical of all villages of the kind, with balconied houses, whose sloping roofs are laden with heavy rocks and ropes against the storms that rage in the winter.

A strangely peaceful-faced people, those of Oberammergau, as if the play around which their whole life centres had touched their souls with the peace of the Christus. During the years between, the men occupy themselves with wood and ivory carving, with tending the great cattle, and with wood-cutting. The women work in their houses, and see to the bringing up of the children, who grow to maturity with the one ideal before them – that of being permitted to appear in the Passion Play which has been played for close on three hundred years.

The Chaletians had been told how it had all begun. How, when a terrible plague had been raging in the district, the people prayed to God that He would deliver them from the pestilence, and when He showed them His infinite mercy, they vowed to commemorate it by acting every ten years the story of that last week in the earthly life of Christ. Thus it has become a tradition, soaked into the flesh and bones of the inhabitants of Oberammergau; embedded in their souls. The most awful thing that can happen to any one of them is to be denied the privilege of appearing in the play. The parts are cast by the priest, and they are prepared by him for their labour of love. The school-children vie with one another in their endeavours to be all they ought to be, lest they are left out of the cast. It can well be imagined, then, how such a life, with such ideals, has affected those who have lived under them always.

The three chief parts are those of the Christus, the Blessed Virgin, and the Magdalene. For three decades the Christus was played by Anton Lang, the wood-carver, whose beautiful face with its strange spirituality has become so familiar to all. The Blessed Virgin is given to the young girl who combines beauty of face with beauty of soul, and both she and the Magdalene must be represented by unmarried girls. Thirty years ago, the girl chosen for the principal woman's part gladly put off her marriage for another year that she might not lose this great boon.

The girls had seen Passion and Miracle plays before, for the people of the Tyrol are deeply religious, and are fond of holding these rites. They themselves performed, every Christmas, a nativity play in aid of the free ward for children at the Sonnalpe sanatorium. They were, therefore, well prepared for what they were to see, and it was a rather graver company than usual that walked down the village street and sought its rooms. Even Jo had forgotten Juliet's story as she glanced from side to side, noting many faces that she would see on the next day in the theatre.

Their guide pointed out various people here and there, and finally the wonderful Anton Lang, who came along with a little child tugging at either hand.

Jo looked at him, and tears came to her eyes. He was an old man now – too old for the part he had filled so marvellously during the three times he had portrayed it. In his kindly blue eyes shone a great peace, and a very tender look was on his face as he answered the chatter of the two little girls with their flaxen pigtails who clung to him, their tongues going at a tremendous rate.

The sweet-faced Virgin was seen later on; and they passed a young girl whom their guide named to them as the Veronica of the play. "It is but a tiny part," he said, gesticulating as he spoke. "When *der Christus* is staggering with His cross along the Via Dolorosa she steps out from the crowd, and offers Him her kerchief to wipe the sweat and blood from His brow. That is all."

"But – very wonderful," said Jo later to Juliet, when they were alone in the narrow room they were to share. "Imagine it, Juliet! I think the hope of being allowed to do just that must make it a great deal easier to be good."

"It isn't easy to be good, whatever hope you have," said Juliet, with a sigh.

"Still, it must be a help," argued Jo.

"Perhaps so. But I expect that girl has just the same struggles as anyone else. It's a difficult world, Joey." Juliet spoke with a little bitterness edging her tones, and Jo said nothing. There was nothing she *could* say.

Luckily, Marie and Frieda came tapping at their door at that moment, to summon them to a meal and to suggest that they should all go for a walk afterwards.

"I want to see the place," said Marie. "The country is so beautiful. And I should like to see the people more, for then they will seem like friends when we go to the theatre tomorrow."

"Very well," agreed Jo. "And if Juliet is with us, I don't suppose anyone will fuss us about supervision."

Juliet laughed. "Well, as I am to be a mistress next term, I should think they would say that you *were* under supervision. Anyway, you're prees, you folk. All right, we'll go. Anyone know what time we feed?"

"Now," said Marie. "We have come to call you."

"I didn't mean that. I meant later on."

Marie shook her head. "I have no idea. But someone will tell us downstairs. We shall not be so long as that, Juliet."

"You don't know," replied Juliet, as she tucked a clean handkerchief into her pocket. "If Jo starts her history-dreaming, we may be stuck for the night."

"Shame!" cried Jo. "I never dream to that extent!"

The elder girl laughed. "Oh, I've know you do some mad things at times when you had gone down the centuries. – Stop it, Joey!"

Jo merely made a wild grab at the plaits that crowned her head, and Juliet had a hard struggle to defend them. Finally, she got away, and tore downstairs to the *Speisesaal*, where she felt that she would be safe from vengeance, since Mademoiselle would be there. The three schoolgirls followed her and took their places demurely at table. Jo leant across when grace had been said, and touched her. "Don't think you've escaped. It's only put off."

"Joey; sit up!" said Juliet. "You can't stretch over like that – it isn't done."

Jo sat up, and the meal went on quietly. There were twelve of them in this house, as well as Mademoiselle and Juliet. The others were scattered through the village, a mistress to each group. Most of them, however, were at the hotel of Herr Mayerl, along with Miss Stewart and Mademoiselle Lachenais. After the meal, the girls were given permission to go out, so long as they kept in parties of not less than four, and kept to the main street of the village and its environs.

"But do not wander further, *mes enfants*," said Mademoiselle Lepâttre. "We must know where we can find you, should we need you in haste."

Joey, Frieda, and Marie got their hats, for the sun was very hot, and joined Juliet in the narrow doorway, where she was chatting to their kind hostess, one Frau Gitterl. She told them with pride that her three daughters were among the throng that weep for the Christ as He passes along the Via Dolorosa; and that her sons were Roman soldiers. Even the two tinies were in the children's chorus.

"It must be very wonderful," said Joey wistfully, "to have the chance of that coming to you!"

The kindly woman smiled. "It is the dream of all our maidens to be fair enough and good enough to be chosen for a speaking part in the play," she said. "And our lads all pray that they may, some day, be permitted to be one of our Lord's Apostles. But not Judas – never that!"

"I can understand that," said Juliet.

"Why, see you, last time, the Judas had to be guarded as he went about the streets, for the people in their fury would have harmed him. And he is a good man, too."

"And the St John?" asked Joey.

She pointed out a tall young fellow coming towards them. Dark hair hung long and crisp about his shoulders; his eyes were full of dreams. "That is he."

They looked at him with a little wonder. It was a very beautiful face, with something of that spirit in it that had moved the real Christ to call St John and his brother the "Sons of Thunder" when in their wrath they would have had Him call down fire from Heaven on the village that received Him not; albeit, it was the face of a dreamer.

"Hans Lang," said their hostess. "He carves in ivory during the other years. And yonder go Aloïs Schmidt and Josef Führer, the St Andrew and the St Thomas. I have a feeling for that one," she went on. "He loved so much, and yet had such fear and unfaith."

"And he died so gloriously," said Joey. "He was martyred in India where he went to teach the Faith."

"Ah well! The Spirit of God can do great marvels – even make one as doubting as he a great martyr," smiled Frau Gitterl. Then she murmured something about the work to be done, and left them to take their walk.

They strolled slowly up the village, encountering Simone, Vanna, and Bianca on their way. These three joined them, and together they walked to the theatre.

"I can scarcely wait till tomorrow," sighed Vanna, as they surveyed the building with its rough wooden fences.

"Nor I," agreed Frieda. "They say there is Mass to be said in the church before the performance. Shall we go?"

"We ought," said Marie. "Yes; let us go."

"I'll come with you," remarked Jo. "There isn't a service of our own; but it's all the same, really."

"Come, then," said Simone. "Madame will not mind."

"Not she! She lets me do as I like about that sort of thing."

So it was arranged; and when they had seen all there was to see of the theatre and the village, Jo suggested that they should strike off through the meadows towards a little stream that ran babbling to itself at the further side.

"These mountains aren't a scrap like ours," she said, "but I like them for a change."

She looked at the mountains with their green forests rising to the summits, and the wide pasture-land at their feet. It was a green and pleasant land, this land of the Passion Play, with a peace in it that was lacking in their own limestone-ringed district. Across the field, carrying to them on the still summer air, came the sound of a boy's strong voice, uplifted in a song which, on the next day, they recognized. A lark mounted up, its notes falling like jewelled rain from the blue sky. The tinkle-tinkle of cowbells sounded in the distance. There was a faint skirl of merry, childish laughter from the banks of the stream, where some children were paddling in the cool waters.

Jo stooped and gathered two or three of the tiny heartsease flowers that spring everywhere in this district. "Heartsease!" she said. "I shall take them home as a memory of this time."

Juliet held out her hand. "Give me some, Jo. I need heartsease."

Jo put the whole cluster into her fingers. "Take them. I can get some more."

She ran off, and presently came back, her hands full of the tiny, butterfly flowers, which she shared with the others.

"Heartsease from this place," said Simone softly. "How beautiful."

They turned back after that. They might be in the thrall of Oberammergau, but they were very human girls, with human appetites, and they felt that it was time for *Kaffee und Kuchen*.

"Though I bet it's only *Butterbrod*," said Jo sagely.

"That might have been thirty odd years ago," returned Juliet. "You forget that America has discovered this now, Joey. I expect we'll get our cakes all right. The Americans are demons for their comfort. They are trying to commercialize even this lovely, sacred thing."

"Trust them!" retorted Jo uncharitably.

"It is well for you that Cornelia and Evvy aren't here," laughed Marie. "They would have something to say to that."

"I say!" Jo suddenly stopped in the middle of the road. "Where *are* those two? I haven't seen a sign of them since we were decanted at the station. Has anyone else?"

"They had *Mittagessen* with us," said Simone. "I think they went out with Carla and Elsie and Anne."

"What! Was Carla the only pree with them? Then come on, you folk! We simply must find them! I'm surprised at Charlie! She knows what they are like by this time, I should think!" And Jo whirled about, bumping into Frieda as she did so.

"Be careful, Joey!" cried Juliet, as she steadied the other girl. "Knocking people over won't help things at all. And I don't suppose Corney and Evvy will have got into much mischief this afternoon. They *can* be good on occasion, you know."

"Yes – on occasion!" retorted Jo. "It is very much on occasion!"

"They will be quite likely to have done something awful," agreed Frieda. "We were bad enough, I know, Juliet. But at least we were never quite so bad as they are."

"I don't know," argued Juliet. "Oh, I don't say *you* were; and Marie had Wanda to look after her. But first and last, you can't say that Jo's school career has been a peaceful one, can you? When she hasn't been doing her level best to kill herself, she has been evolving some mad mischief which no one could foresee and forbid before it was done. I'll grant you originality, Jo. But the wonder is my hair didn't turn grey over some of your pranks!"

But Jo was too full of what the American couple might have been doing to answer this insult. She hurried down the street to the hotel, and ran up to Miss Stewart's room, to find that lady out. All the same, as events proved, she was quite right in her anticipations. Before evening, the village was ringing with excitement, and the Chalet School had to admit that Corney and Evvy had done it once again!

CHAPTER XIV

The Sensation

As EVERYONE SAID AFTERWARDS, IT was just what might have been expected.

"Why ever did we let those wretched children go out without dog-collars and chains?" cried Miss Stewart in exasperated tones. "Whenever the Middles are let loose they always contrive to do something they ought not!"

"Quite true," said Miss Wilson. "Don't look so righteous, you prefects. You used to be quite as bad – and I'm not sure that some of you are much improved, even now," she added.

"But to create a sensation like that! And *here*!" groaned Jo, regardless of the last thrust. "I should have thought that even Evvy and her crew could have managed to behave decently *here*!"

"I feel inclined to take all of you home," declared Mademoiselle in her own language. "If it had been only one – or two! But five of them!"

"You will not refuse to let them see the Play tomorrow, will you, Mademoiselle?" pleaded Frieda, true to her name's meaning as always. "Indeed, they are very sorry, and are in great trouble lest you should think them unfit for it."

Mademoiselle smiled slowly. "No; I shall not do that, Frieda. That would be too heavy a punishment for them. But they must understand that they will not be trusted to be alone for the rest of the time that we are here. Always, they must have someone with them to supervise their acts. We cannot trust them."

"It was only mischief," pleaded Jo.

"True. But it should not have been even that."

So the fiat went forth that Evadne, Cornelia, Elsie, Maria, and Ilonka were not to be allowed to go about alone. They must always be with either a mistress or a prefect; and bitterly they rued the wild impulse that had taken them when they had disgraced themselves, and, as Mademoiselle told them sadly, their school. They minded that almost more than their punishment. And be very sure that the rest of the school did not forget to call them to account for what they had done. However, this is hurrying on too quickly. The full story of the exploits of "Those wretched Middles", as Joey called them, is best told in that young lady's own words, in a letter she sent to her sister the next day.

Dearest Madge,

What you will say when you read this is more than I can imagine. I expect you will be furious at first. I was! But I've got more or less over it now, and can laugh, though I don't let them see me doing so. It's those Middles again. Charlie says that whenever there is trouble it's always the Middles. She and Bill were positively insulting about us when we were Middles. We certainly never did the mad things that Evvy and Co. do!"

Of course all the staff are wild, but I think those young beauties will behave themselves for the future. Here's the whole story for you to judge for yourself.

In the afternoon – we reached Oberammergau just in time for Mittagessen – we all got permission to go out provided we went in groups. Juliet, Frieda, Simone, Marie, and I foregathered, and had a gorgeous time, walking about the place, and seeing all we could. Just before time for Kaffee und Kuchen someone suggested that we ought to see what the kids were doing. We all know what Evvy and Corney are, and just how much they are to be trusted. Someone said that Carla was the only pree with them; and Carla! She's a dear, but she can't keep order with those young imps. When we got back to the hotel where they were supposed to be parked we found that Carla had come back with a headache, and no one knew where the kids were. Charlie was out with someone else – I believe she had taken some of the Juniors for a trot; and there were the quintet all to themselves. They had even left Anne Seymour, who had been with them at first – we found her sketching further down the street. We divided forces after that, Frieda and Marie going one way, Simone and I another, Juliet another, and Vanna and Bianca – I forgot to tell you that they were there, too – a fourth. Simone and I found them – we would have that luck!

Madge, you never saw five such little sights in your life! Elsie was soaking wet; Evvy wasn't much better; and the other three were in rags – literally! In addition to all this, their faces were painted with designs that would have made the most modern of modern artists green with envy. We didn't waste any time over finding out the reason for this lovely exhibition. Besides, there was a large enough crowd as it was. I should think half the grown-ups and all the children of Oberammergau were there, with a few visitors of most nations thrown in for luck. That's what it felt like at any rate. Simone closed up on one side, and I on the other, and we marched them back to the hotel in dead silence. Even Corney seemed subdued. I think they hadn't bargained for such an audience.

Charlie was in by the time we got them back, and her face when she saw them was a picture! Ilonka and Maria were crying by this time, and I don't think the other three were far off it. They knew what they'd done all right, and they knew that they would have to pay for their fun now.

Charlie opened her lips at length, and let one sentence drop – that's the effect she gave anyhow. "Go and wash, and make yourselves decent in appearance."

They went, and we went with them to be sure that they did what they were told, and no more. They washed, and we washed! Their luckless faces were scrubbed till they were nearly red raw, and still the colour wouldn't come off! I began to feel desperate. Juliet had joined us by this time, and Charlie, and we couldn't make any impression on the blobs and squirls with which they had decorated themselves. I did suggest scrubbing brushes, but Charlie said she thought we didn't need to be quite so drastic as all that. Finally, some brain said "Turpentine!" We acted on it, and finally we found that the streaks were beginning to fade a bit. It took half-an-hour's good work to get most of it clear, and even then there were signs of what had happened. As for their skins, parboiled is the only word that describes them!

When we got through the cleansing processes, and they all looked more or less like Christians again, they were hauled before an informal court of justice to hear what they had to say for themselves. In fact there were two. The staff had first go; we came in second. I think, of the two, they preferred the staff. After a lot of nonsense, this is what we got out of them, and I hope you think they behaved like girls who are nearly fifteen!

They went for a walk, but found things on the dull side. So some bright soul – Evvy for a ducat! – suggested they should turn off into the fields, and go to the stream. Well, there was nothing wrong in that. We did it ourselves. They were all stockingless, of course. We all shed our stockings as soon as we had left the train. No one thinks anything of it, as you know. I overheard one or two remarks from visitors as we went up the street, but didn't pay any attention to them.

For a while they seemed to have contented themselves with paddling in the stream, and splashing round generally. Then they tired of that. They sat down near some bushes, and Evvy and Corney began to swap yarns about America in the days of the Pilgrim Fathers. So far as I can gather, they tried to outdo each other, and some of the things they appear to have recounted to the other three were enough to make your hair curl – if it didn't do it naturally already. Elsie, I think, had a little more sense than to believe them, but Marie and Ilonka simply sat with their mouths open, swallowing everything whole.

Evvy says it was fun at first, but they got bored with it, and then Lonny was moved, in an evil moment, to think of acting what they had just heard. It sounds ridiculous for girls of their ages, but the idea appealed to them – it would! Corney and Evvy immediately decided to play at Captain John Smith and Pocahontas. And just here was where Evvy had the nerve to say, "It's your fault, Jo. You told us about them first."

I squashed her good and hard, remarking that, of course, I never thought they'd be so childish as to play at Red Indians because I'd told them a true story.

Then Corney said, "Well, you always say that the best way to learn history is to act it."

Those monkeys are too sharp for words. Were we ever really as bad as that, Madge?

Having decided to act the story, they did their best to dress it. They couldn't get hold of any feathers – luckily! – but they knew where Anne had put her oil-colour box which she had brought with her. Why on earth she couldn't have wanted it for the afternoon I can't think! She says that she never thought of it, and she wanted to make pencil sketches. She's got a bookful of the loveliest little things to show you when we get back. She really is wonderful at it!

However, to resume! Evvy went for the box, and they used up most of the more lurid colours in adorning themselves. That they've got to pay for, out of their pocket money, so they'll have to go without sweets and fruit for a few weeks. Then they laid the box down in a convenient spot, and forgot all about it till late at night, when Anne suddenly asked where it was. Mercifully, it had been found, and was brought round next day, none the worse, except that it was three parts empty, thanks to their having been Red Indians! Elsie, as the captain, did not paint her face, but she imitated tattooing marks all over her arms and cheeks, and used up every scrap of cobalt Anne possessed. She has a greyish look even now! Then they began. They seem to have raised the place with their war-whoops, and generally behaved like mad things, till Elsie fell into the stream. That cooled their ardour a little, and then they suddenly realized that they had a large audience watching them. It was at this point that Elsie, who certainly possesses most of the common sense of the five, jumped at what they had done and, to quote herself, nearly swooned with horror. She stopped the game at once, and they made tracks for home, hoping to get there safely, and get themselves made decent without being caught. Lonny declares they would have owned up afterwards, and I believe her. They're a wicked set, but they're sporting enough. Of course, it was a hopeless job, and they were caught most thoroughly, for they ran into our arms, just as they were beginning to have a little hope of getting away with it.

That's the story. You asked me when I was last up what I thought would happen next. Well, I might have thought of a good many things; but never that. One mercy, they are all so subdued that they are like lambs. Long may it last! They were afraid, even after Mademoiselle had said that they might see the Play, that the authorities would not let them in. However, nothing has been said about it, and they went with the crowd of us.

As for the Play, I can't write it here. For one thing, I haven't recovered from it yet. For another, even talking it will be difficult. I'll do my best when I see you, though, and the Robin will be sure to want to know all about it. It is the most wonderful thing I have ever seen, or ever expect to see.

We will be back on Tuesday, so all further news then.
Love to you all from us.
Jo.

P.S. – Will you try to let Gisela know about Maria's share of the business before we come? She has just been in to ask me. She knows that Gisela will be furious, and I think she hopes the edge of the fury will have worn off a bit if she knows as soon as possible.

CHAPTER XV

The Passion Play

ON THE SUNDAY MORNING THE girls got up early. Many of them went to hear Mass at the village church; the rest went for a walk. Jo went with Frieda and Marie, for she was accustomed to going sometimes at the Tiernsee, Mrs Russell having no prejudices against it. After Mass the girls returned to *Frühstück* with fine appetites for the rolls and coffee which were set before them. After that it was a case of getting up and hurrying off to get their seats, for the Play begins at eight o'clock, and goes on till six p.m., with a two hours' break at noon for lunch.

They found it a bit of a rush, as Jo genially remarked when she was finally settled in her seat, with Simone the faithful on one side, Juliet on the other, and Marie and Frieda in front. The Chalet School made quite a good showing of it as they sat in their solid block, and many were the interested looks directed at them as they sat there. They were early, so Jo looked round, and promptly scandalized Mademoiselle's sense of the proprieties by exclaiming, "Goodness! There's the Stuffer and Maria! Well I never!"

The two ladies at whom her cry was directed looked up at this, and promptly became all beams and nods. They were elderly, clad as the Continental humorous papers invariably portray the English tourist, and looked as if they would have been more at home in an English cathedral town than in a little village in the Mittenwald. But that they were overjoyed at seeing Jo was evident.

"Just imagine!" remarked Jo, when she had waved a friendly greeting at the pair, and was sitting quietly in her place again. "We haven't seen them since that garden party of ours at the end of Grizel's last term. Where is Grizel? – Grizel! Have you see who's here?"

Pretty, self-sufficient Grizel Cochrane looked across to the couple at whom Jo was pointing with a complete lack of manners, and her eyes widened. "*Those* two!" she exclaimed. "Why, they are the last I should have expected to see here!"

"Now I shouldn't," replied Jo. "It's just what I *should* expect. They are confirmed globe-trotters, as we know. This is just where I *should* have expected to meet them, if I'd given a thought to it."

What more might have been said on the subject was lost, for at that moment the Chorus entered to take up their position, and the Choragus, or Leader of the Chorus, began the intoning with which the Play opens. This was followed by a tableau showing the Expulsion from Eden, while the Chorus sang an anthem. Then there was a little silence, and the Prologue, spoken by Anton Lang, the famous Christus, rang out under the blue summer sky. The old man's voice made the guttural German sound musical as he rolled out his words, and the girls were spellbound. A second tableau, the Adoration of the Cross, followed, and then there was a rustle as people settled themselves finally. The Play proper now began.

It opens at the Entry into Jerusalem, and is heralded by a great chorus of many singers. Children ran to strew their palms before the Christ, and the girls were agreeably thrilled to recognize many of them. The second scene shows the Cleansing of the Temple, and as the homely German sentences floated across the great auditorium to them the incidents of the Last Week became more vivid and real to the girls than ever before. The fury of the Jewish traders, as their tables were overthrown; the flight of the white doves, as the Christ released them and they fluttered up to the sky; the beautiful face of the man chosen to play the greatest part in the world; all brought home the poignancy of the story to them better than any other thing. Jo sat in a spellbound silence as the story unfolded itself to the end of the first act. Then she sat back in her seat, heaving a sigh of pleasure.

"What comes next?" demanded Cornelia Flower, leaning over to poke her.

"Couldn't say," replied the head girl. "Oh, see! The Chorus are coming again. That means more music. They sing gorgeously, don't they?"

"They sure do," affirmed Evadne, who was not far from her fellow countrywoman. "It's a pity Plato isn't here. He'd be all over them."

Jo reflected that their eccentric singing master would have been thrilled at the singing. A keen musician himself, he had trained the girls of the Chalet School not only in singing, as he was fully competent to do, but in appreciation of good singing. The sweet voices of the choir, showing their careful preparation, would have rejoiced his heart.

"Is Plato as mad as ever?" asked Grizel Cochrane of Carla, who sat beside her.

There was a hardness in the character of Grizel Cochrane which her early training had done little to eradicate. Indeed, she would have been worse than she was had it not been for her years at the Chalet School, where they had done their best to soften this stony nature. Carla, deeply devotional as many of the Tyrolese are, was too much wrapped up in the Play to heed the flippant question, and Grizel, with a shrug of her graceful shoulders, sank into silence again, as the beautiful voices welled up again on the summer air.

The Chorus was followed by a tableau, and then came the council of the priests and the scribes, with Caiaphas directing events to the Crucifixion. The actor was marvellous in his diction and the fervour he put into the part. Throughout this act he dominates the stage, and his strong, stern face above the priestly vestments showed well.

All through the long, hot morning they sat, watching the scenes in almost utter silence. Even Evadne and Cornelia, the wildest pair in the school, were awed into silence. Through the many scenes – the feast in the house of Simon the Leper, where Judas protests at the waste of the precious spikenard; the Weeping over Jerusalem; the conventions among the angry priests; the final consent to the great betrayal – all these lived for the school, and for many others, as the hours passed on and the sun continued his journey across the sky. It came as a shock when the act ended, and there was a break. Jo, visibly much affected, remained silent the whole time. Her eyes were glowing with a deep, inward glow as of one who sees a vision. Frieda was the same. One or two of the others showed the same absorption. Juliet had forgotten her own trouble for the time being, and was thinking of what was to follow. Even the little ones were stilled.

"It is very wonderful," said Miss Stewart, who was sitting with Cornelia and Evadne, one each side of her. "I am glad we are seeing it."

"Guess I am," said Evadne in subdued tones. "I wouldn't have missed it for pie! Say, Miss Stewart, why don't they do things like this at home? Guess it's a long way better than everlasting sermons on Sunday."

"Because the people here are simpler, Evadne," said Grizel, who was behind them and had heard her question. "In America, you are all too sophisticated to think of such a thing."

"We ain't!" retorted Cornelia, who had no idea what the term meant, and was not going to hear her countrymen maligned if she could help it. "We're just as good as the next – so there, Grizel Cochrane!"

Grizel laughed. "I wasn't saying you weren't. Only that your people are not – not childlike enough to feel the great help that such things as the Passion Play are to the people here."

The third act shows the parting at Bethany from Simon the Leper, and the farewell of Christ to His mother. The Virgin was played with an exquisite simplicity and pathos which moved the girls almost to tears. The Magdalene was bolder in treatment, but still with that strange touch of innocence that is rarely seen in any of the professional theatres.

Act Four, after the opening chorus, begins with the tableau showing the rejection of Vashti, and the acceptance of Esther as Queen. While it was in progress the choir sang the magnificent "Jerusalem, Jerusalem, Awake!" with its thrilling harmonies. And so the Play passed on to the seducing of Iscariot to the betrayal of his master. The Last Supper, with all its poignant wording and the great teaching, kept the girls very quiet. Even the two small Americans had subsided, and were wet-eyed when it ended.

By this time the sun was high in the sky, and the Play was delayed for the two hours of rest and refreshment that are as necessary to the audience as to the players. The strain of the Play is enormous, whether one is a mere spectator or an actor. Some of the girls were feeling worn out, and Mademoiselle, once she had got her flock safely gathered together outside the theatre, gave orders that after *Mittagessen* they were to rest for half an hour before they returned to witness the final scenes. One or two of the more restless spirits grumbled at this; but the majority were thankful to hear it. After a good meal, Joey and Juliet retired to their room, and there was silence through the village, save for the occasional voices of tourists who had to do much in little time, and the summer sounds that drifted to the girls through the open windows.

Finally they arose again, feeling all the better for the short rest, and made their way through the heat back to their seats. The buying of Judas, which filled the next act, passed quickly; then came the great scene in the garden, with the sleeping disciples, so anxious to do what they might for their master; so pitiably weak in the hour of trial. Finally, the arrival of the armed bands and the priests, led by Iscariot to the Christ, brought the scene to a close, with the jeering of the traders, scribes, and priests' servants.

The trial before the High Priest and the Sanhedrim came next, and it was followed by the denial of St Peter. So they came to the trial before Pilate, with his pathetic wavering to and fro – his longing to release one whom he knew to be innocent, while, for fear of the Jewish priests, he dared not. The mocking by King Herod; the refusal of Pilate to pass sentence of death on the man in whom he found no wrong; the accusation of the priests that the Roman governor was no true servant to Caesar; the mockery of the Roman soldiers – all were repeated with all the sincerity of which the people of Oberammergau were capable. By this time many people in the audience were in tears, and there was a deathly hush under the calm summer sky.

There came the final scenes – the choice of Barabbas, rather than the Christ; the walk to Calvary; the raising of the Cross; the final words, and the death.

Knowing the emotional natures of many of the girls, Mademoiselle glanced uneasily along the rows. Many of them were sobbing; others were biting their lips. Joey sat in silence, her face white with the strain, her eyes wide. Only when the Virgin took the body of the Son in her arms did a sound break from her – a little strangled sob.

Then came the visit of the women to the garden; the discovery of the stone rolled away; the final tableaux; the last chorus with its triumphal "Hallelujah!" The stage cleared; the Play was ended. Slowly the vast audience rose and began to make its way out. Mademoiselle marshalled the girls into their lines, and marched them to their various lodgings. Her eye was on Joey, whose white face worried her. However, Jo reached the house in safety. She went upstairs with Juliet, who remained silent. They were all still under the spell of the Play. Suddenly Mademoiselle, coming to the door, heard an exclamation of horror from the elder girl. Opening, she went in quickly, in time to see Juliet catch a grey-faced Joey and lower her gently to the floor. The strain had been too great, and the head girl had fainted.

CHAPTER XVI

The Middles' Latest

IT WAS GENERALLY ANTICIPATED THAT trouble must come from the Middles at least once a week. They were not behindhand in the matter of ingenuity, and they were as full of original sin as most people of their age. But it is safe to say that no one had ever anticipated such a thing as their next outbreak turned out to be.

It happened a week after the return from Oberammergau. For the whole of that week the school had been more or less subdued. The influence of the Play lasted all that time. After that it was high time for the unruly members of the school to get into trouble of some sort or another, and staff and prefects alike awaited their new villainy with some anxiety.

"Goodness knows what it will be," said Jo Bettany, discussing that matter in the august assembly of the prefects' meeting. "What haven't they done that they *could* do yet?"

"Nothing, I should think," replied Marie von Eschenau.

"Oh, there must be a few things they haven't done," said Frieda. They were all talking in German. "They haven't burnt down the school yet, for instance."

"They aren't given much chance of that, with electric light everywhere and the big stoves for warmth," said Jo, with a grin. "And they aren't likely to try a flood, since Elsie and Anne got into such a row over leaving the bath-taps running that day we had fire-drill."

"That was funny," laughed Simone, her grave little face brightening as she remembered the incident.

"It was funny to see Charlie and Bill trying to pick their way through a meander of soapy water in a hurry." chuckled Jo.

"What is there left that they can do?" asked Carla.

"Well, they might try a midnight. We've none of us ever run to that," said the head girl thoughtfully.

"Somehow it never struck us that we ought to keep in line there with the books," said Marie. "We always have such super food that we never want anything extra."

"It is strange," agreed Simone, "for we always used to try to be quite like the books."

When they came to think of it, it *was* strange, and no one could explain it, so they dropped the subject and went on to something else. And then the Middles' outburst came, and was so original that they were all rendered breathless by it.

It began on a glorious day at the end of June, when the girls had been released from school half an hour earlier than usual. There were so many weeks in winter when they could not get out, owing to the severity of the weather, that the staff made a point of seeing to it that they got as much fresh air as possible in the summer. Thus the Middles, free from their tasks, rioted out to the playing field that surrounded the two chalets which formed the school.

Maria Marani, Cornelia Flower, Evadne Lannis, Elsie Carr, Margia Stevens, and Ilonka Barkocz wandered over to the far side of the field, which adjoined the foot-path that ran by the way to the Tiern Pass. Here they climbed up on to the top of the fence – a strictly forbidden thing – and settled down to chat. They had not been there very long when a sound of loud sobs disturbed them.

They all turned to look over the fence, and beneath them saw a small girl of about ten. Her thick black hair was gathered in two pigtails which hung down to her waist; her brown arms and feet were bare and dusty, and a great blister crossed one toe; her round, olive-hued face was stained and swollen with tears, and her clothes were in rags. Altogether it would have been difficult to find a more forlorn little specimen of humanity. The Chalet girls looked at one another in discomfort. She was obviously in great distress and, as Margia said later, they somehow felt pigs to be so happy and carefree themselves when anyone so much younger than they was in such trouble. Presently, overcoming her sudden shyness, the leader of the Middles bent down. "*Mädchen*," she began, speaking in German, since they all thought the child was a Tyrolean.

The little girl started violently and looked up, raising a pair of vividly blue eyes to theirs. For a moment she stared at them as if she could scarcely believe her senses. Then she spoke, and it was their turn to get a shock; for in the purest of Irish brogues, she exclaimed, "Holy Saints preserve us! An' who might *ye* be?"

When they had recovered, Elsie spoke. "Why are you crying?" she asked.

The small stranger shook back the loose tendrils of hair from her face and tossed her head defiantly. "Oi amn't!" she retorted, though the tears were still trickling down her face.

"What d'you call it then?" asked Margia with interest.

The child changed her tactics, "An' if Oi am, phwat's it to do wid ye?" she demanded.

"Nothing – but we do not like to see one like you in sorrow," said Ilonka, her English becoming careful from shyness.

The child suddenly flung up her arms. "Oh, wirra, wirra! An' niver a truer wurrd ye spake!" she cried. "'Tis in desperate bad sorrow Oi am, an' niver a one to care at all – at all!"

The Middles looked at each other again. Then, with one accord, they swung their legs over the fence, and dropped down to the footpath where their new acquaintance stood. They gathered round her, and Margia, with a violent blush, put an arm round her. "Do tell us, dear," she urged. "*We* care – honest Injun we do."

The child, who had fallen again to her sobbing, lifted her face from her hands to look at them in amazement. "How can ye care?" she asked. "Sure, ye never saw me before."

"Of course we care!" cried Elsie. "D'you think we're heathen? Tell us what's wrong. Has anyone been hurting you, or anything?"

"Where d'you hail from?" asked Cornelia, speaking for the first time.

"And what's your handle?" added Evadne.

"I vote we sit down over there on that log," said Margia.

Regardless of the fact that they were breaking rules right and left, the Middles escorted their find over to the aforesaid log, and presently they were all squatting on it or before it, the child in their midst. "Me name's Bridget O'Ryan," she said, with a hiccup. "Oi'm from County Kerry – 'tis there Oi was born."

"But how on earth did you get here?" demanded Margia.

"Sure, Oi came wid me ma. Me da died, an' me ma came wid Miss Honora from the Castle as maid, bekase she had been that before she and me da had it med up to marry, Miss Honora said to bring me too. Miss Honora died, she did, two years back, and me ma married Luigi Desti, that was Miss Honora's chauffeur – sure, wasn't he pestering her to do that same all the toime?"

"Then where are they now?" asked Evadne.

Bridget burst into loud wails again. "'Tis dead they are, may their souls rest in peace!" she sobbed. "Me ma died whin the babby come, an' Luigi, he died last week. His sister, she come, an' said she would take the babby, for 'twas her brother's. But me, that's no kin to her, she couldn't take, for she has tin av her own. So they spake to the praste for me, an' he said Oi shud go to the Cecilia Home for Orphans. But Oi'm no beggar – an' me da a soldier! So Oi ran away, an Oi come here. An' now Oi've no money left, an' no place to go, for there isn't any of the O'Ryans left but mesilf. An' what will Oi do at all, at all?"

"Oh, don't begin to cry again!" implored Margia, with a hug. "We can get you something to eat, anyhow, and you can spend the night in the games shed – we could make you quite comfy with a few rugs, I know."

Bridget choked back her sobs, and sat looking at them trustfully. Her short life had been filled with love, as they found later, for the Italian chauffeur had had all his countrymen's love for children, and had made a pet of his wife's first child. Even the arrival of his own little son had made no difference. The big sister who had come after his death, and had refused to take Bridget, had done so reluctantly. She would gladly have brought the child home, but her own large family and the extreme poverty of themselves had made it impossible. She had done the best she could for the little orphan in speaking to the priest, and when she had broken the news of the child's future destination, she had done her best to make it as attractive as possible. But Bridget had the deeply ingrained horror of the Irish peasantry for any kind of charitable institution, and she had finally rebelled, and run away from Hall, where she had been living with her stepfather at the time of his death. How she had ever managed to get as far as the Tiernsee without being found was something they never knew. She had had a few schillings, and since, normally, she was a pretty child, she had not starved. The Chalet girls found all this out after Cornelia had been "boosted" up to the top of the fence again, and dropped down on the other side, to go to the school and see what she could find in the way of food for their new protégée.

"She'd better have clothes, too," said Evadne, surveying her rags critically. "I've got an extra vest that Matey doesn't know about. And there's that old tunic your kid grew out of last term. We could find some tops for her among us, surely, and enough undies for the next week or two?"

Margia, to whom she had more particularly addressed herself, nodded. "It's too hot for that thick tunic now," she said reasonably. "But there's a blue cotton frock Amy's grown out of. Matey's even given it a false hem, and it's nearly up to her neck. She can't wear it again. But Bridget is lots smaller than Amy. I should say it would be just about right for her."

Bridget listened to these plans for her comfort with brightening eyes. She loathed the idea of an institution, but she had no objection to having things made easy for her. So when the Middles rather shyly asked her if she would accept what they offered, she replied with great enthusiasm, "Sure, an' Oi will that! An 'tis yourselves is the good-hearted young ladies to be taking such trouble for me, intoirely! The Holy Saints reward yez for it! An' if there's iver annythin' Biddy O'Ryan can do for yez, ye may be sure she'll do it wid a heart an' half!"

As she finished this speech, Cornelia's hail could be heard from the other side of the fence, and a moment later she reappeared, bearing her spoils in her attaché case. "Some of us must go," she panted, when she had safely rejoined them. "Jo's been yelling all over the place for you, Maria; and Herr Anserl has come up to give you an extra lesson, Margia, and Bill said I was to tell you to go *at once*! She seemed rather ratty about it – got her rag out!" she added pensively.

Margia's face clouded over. "Bother him!" she said ungratefully. "What does he want to do that for? I had a lesson yesterday, and that's enough for one week!"

"Well, you'd better go," replied Cornelia. "I tell you, Bill's mad."

Margia got up from her seat on the log next to Bridget, and pushed the thick, curly hair out of her eyes. "Come on, Maria," she said. – "You'd better come, too, Evvy. The rest must see to Bridget for the time being. We'll be back as soon as we can to arrange about smuggling her into the games shed for the night, and bringing her towels and things. – See if you can get hold of Amy, Elsie, and ask her for the frock. Tell her I said so. – I'll see you later, Bridget."

With that she went up the fence with a monkey-like agility, followed by Maria and Evadne, and the rest, left with their foundling, proceeded to feed her on rolls and fruit, and some cold fish which Cornelia had managed to abstract from the pantry when Luise, who ruled matters in the Chalet kitchen, was looking the other way.

A square meal gave things a different complexion for Bridget. She ate heartily, and the girls noticed that she ate daintily, for all her hunger. The dead mother had been quick to pick up little niceties from her employer, and she had taught her child well. Bridget swallowed the last crumb, and then looked regretfully at her dirty hands and feet. "Oi cud do wid a bath," she said, with a sigh.

The Middles looked at each other again. This was rather a poser. But Bridget saw the way out quickly. "Isn't there a lake yonder?" she said eagerly. "If 'twas the way ye cud be bringin' me somethin' to dhry meself wid,

Oi'd get the grrand bath there intoirely."

"Good scheme!" said Elsie appreciatively. "I'll go and fetch a towel, and some of you get her round without anyone catching us, if you can. – Lonny, you take her. – Don't *you* go, Corney; everyone knows your mop. You get back, and slide over to the flower-garden. You may be able to get out that way."

She got back over the fence, and Cornelia, with a toss of the bright, fair hair that made her rather a conspicuous object, followed her, leaving Ilonka of the brown plaits and more ordinary appearance to escort the little stranger round the fencing that shut off the school grounds from the outside world to the lake-side. Ilonka and her charge got there safely, but Cornelia was caught by Marie von Eschenau, and sent off to play tennis, while Elsie had a very close shave of being found in the dormitory out of hours by Matron. It was only by diving under her bed that she escaped the argus gaze of the school tyrant – though they all loved "Matey", she harried them for the good of their souls at times – and then she had to wait ten minutes before the coast was clear. Finally she contrived to reach the other two in safety, and exhibited her own big bath-towel to the entranced Bridget's gaze.

"Sure, miss," she exclaimed excitedly, "'tis as big as Miss Honora's iver was! An' the scenty soap, too! Oh, but 'tis good yez are to me!"

"It's nothing," said Elsie nonchalantly. "Come on down to the bathing-place – and Lonny, you go back an' see if you can get her some clothes to wear. She can't put on *those* rags again!"

Ilonka contrived to get through the garden and into the house without any difficulty. There she boldly marched into Amy Stevens's dormitory and abstracted from her drawers the frock Margia had mentioned, as well as some necessary underthings. Shoes and stockings she provided from her own store, for she had noticed that Bridget had a well-grown foot. Also, she remembered to take her comb, and some hair-ribbons. So laden, she made her way back to the bathing-place, and found Bridget already bathed, and wrapped in the towel, her magnificent hair spread out over her shoulders, drying in the sun.

"Good-o!" said Elsie, when she saw the comb and ribbons. "No, Biddy, here's your clothes. Trot in there, and get into them. Can you manage with your wet hair?"

For reply, Bridget hastily twisted up her locks and tucked them firmly under her chin. Then she vanished, and ten minutes later came out, looking considerably better. Her shoes and stockings she still carried in her hand, and she had donned the towel again to keep the wet hair off the frock.

"If ye'd be excusin' me wearin' the shoes an' stockings, miss," she said, "Oi'd be obliged to yez. My feet are sore for thim."

"Oh, well, lots of people go barefoot here in summer," said Elsie.

"We do at times," added Ilonka.

"I wonder where Corney's got to?" Elsie looked round anxiously.

"She has been caught, perhaps," suggested Ilonka.

"Quite likely. I do wish those wretched prees would mind their own business sometimes!"

"Well, what are we to do with Bridget until bedtime?" asked the Hungarian girl practically. "We cannot take her to the games shed yet, for it will be in use until seven o'clock."

There was a hasty consultation, and they finally decided that Bridget must go to the pine woods and stay there till the evening. They had three schillings between them, and this would buy her a little food. There was some fruit left from Cornelia's raid, and she would be all right for the present. Whoever came to take her to the games shed must bring her something for the night, and they would let her out first thing in the morning. Bridget had known so much change during the past few weeks that she accepted their decisions with equanimity. She agreed to hide in the woods, and she could always ask the time when she thought it was getting near bedtime for her benefactresses. She ran off, her old rags under her arm, for she had agreed to bury them somewhere under a log, as they obviously could not stay in the bathing-house. She had just gone when the two Middles heard the sound of familiar voices, and realized, to their horror, that some of the Seniors were going to take advantage of the hot afternoon and bathe.

"Horrors!" gasped Elsie. "There'll be an awful fuss!"

Ilonka, practical as ever, caught her hand, and dragged her away without a word. Round the opposite side of the bathing-house they went, and crouched down behind one of the Chalet boats which were drawn up there on a little slipway. Just in time too; for the next minute a selection of the Fifth and Sixth, headed by Jo Bettany, Frieda Mensch, and Carla von Flügen hove in sight, and ran round to the bathing-house door. An exclamation from Jo at the state of the floor – Biddy had dripped thoroughly – reached the guilty pair. They dared say nothing till the Seniors were all in, and then they rose from their hiding place and fled up the garden path, luckily reaching the haven of the playing fields without being caught. Once there, Elsie faced round on Ilonka. "Lonny! They'll see the drips! What on earth are we to do?"

CHAPTER XVII

A Mystery

THE SENIORS WERE CERTAINLY SURPRISED to find the floor of the bathing-house liberally bespattered with water. No one had used it since the previous evening, so far as they knew, and, as Jo said, the heat of the day would certainly have dried up any water from the day before. "*Have* any of the kids been bathing?" she demanded of the others.

Carla shook her head. "No; I am sure they have not. Do you not remember, my Jo, that Mademoiselle said we must come quietly, as she had not permitted the Middles to bathe today, as it was so very hot, she feared lest they might be ill."

"Query," said Anne, with a grin. "Why should they perhaps be ill, and us not?"

"We've got more sense than they have," said Joey shortly. "Never mind about that. What I want to know is, who has been using our bathing-house? They've got a nerve, whoever it is. Besides, I thought it was locked. It generally is."

"Do you not remember?" said Frieda. "Mademoiselle had it unlocked because Charlie and Bill were bathing earlier this afternoon. I saw them coming down while we were having singing."

"Then that explains that," said Jo. "But it doesn't explain how the floor got into *this* mess. I'm sure they never did it. They always sit in the sun and dry off after they come out – I've seen them at it."

It was a mystery, and one which they couldn't solve. The Seniors gave it up for the time being and had their bathe. But when it was over, and they were all met in the garden for *Kaffee und Kuchen*, Jo returned to the subject once more. "Could it have been those Middles?" she asked her own set, as they lounged in deck-chairs, drinking their iced coffee, and munching little twists of fancy bread.

"What?" asked Frieda. "Oh, you mean that mess in the bathing-house? I do not see how they could have anything to do with it. We know that they were all in the playing fields—"

"Some of them had to be sent for," broke in Marie. "And where was Margia all afternoon, Jo?"

"Music lesson," replied Jo, with her mouth full. "Herr Anserl came up to give her an extra one. Goodness knows why. I expect the kid was mad about it. She thought she was going to get a free afternoon."

"Who had to be sent for?" asked Frieda.

"Oh, the usual crowd – Evvy, Corney, Lonny, Elsie – I don't know who else."

"That set are always in mischief," observed Carla. "Where had they been, Jo?"

"Didn't ask. Some hidey-hole of their own."

Simone looked up. "Maria was one of them, my Jo. She came late to the field and she looked hot and untidy."

Jo raised her eyebrows. "That's something new for Maria. She generally looks as though she'd just stepped out of a band-box."

"Even so she could scarcely have been bathing," said Marie. "There was not the time. And her hair was quite dry when I saw her."

"Then it must have been some outsiders – and they jolly well *were* outsiders to use our bathing-house like that," said Jo. "Cheek, I call it!"

At this point Juliet Carrick, who had been spending the week up at the Sonnalpe, came quietly into the garden, where she was greeted by rapturous cries from the elder girls. With her was Grizel Cochrane, who had been with her, and who was spending the summer vacation at the Tiernsee. With one accord the Sixth arose and pulled the newcomers into chairs, and plied them with coffee and fancy bread before they were allowed to speak. As soon as they were supplied, and the Seniors had resettled themselves, Jo asked her unvarying question. "How's the Robin?"

"Better," replied Juliet. "They think it's all safe, Jo; so don't worry, old thing. Madame is splendid; and Davie is beginning to get about all over. Dr Jem is coming down early on Sunday morning to take you and Marie up there. – Marie, I've got some news for you. Who do you think is coming to the Sonnalpe next month?"

"Not Wanda?" Marie sounded incredulous.

Juliet nodded. "Yes; Friedel has got leave, so he is bringing Wanda and little Kurt to us for the rest of the summer to buck her up. The letter came for Dr Jem yesterday morning."

"Is she not so well?" asked Marie, her eyes widening.

"Rather tried by the summer heats – you know what it can be like in Vienna. They think she will get on more quickly up there where it's cooler, and they get all the breezes."

"And the twins?" asked Frieda, with a smile.

"Imps!" said Grizel tersely. "The sooner that young monkey Rix gets to school the better. He's in mischief all day long, and Peggy is very nearly as bad. They keep the house lively, I can assure you!"

"And what about Stacie?" asked Simone. "Can she yet sit up?"

"Your English!" Grizel laughed. "When do you mean to speak correctly, Simone? You've had five years here, and you still speak it like a foreigner."

Simone flushed, and darted a resentful look at the speaker. Grizel Cochrane was little given to heed the feelings of others. She was greatly improved since the day when she had first come out to the Tyrol, five years before; but she was still Grizel.

Jo saw the look, and slipped a consoling arm through her friend's. "You haven't told us about Stacie yet," she reminded the elder girl. "And what's the news of Gisela and Baby Natalie?"

"Stacie is in a sitting position for most of the day now," said Juliet. "Gisela is very well, and Baby Natalie is a darling. – No, thank you, Carla. I couldn't eat another thing. And there is a limit to everything – even to the amount of iced coffee once can drink on a boiling hot day. What happens this evening, anyone? No prep, of course."

"Practice for the boat race," said Marie. "It takes place in three weeks' time, and we must beat the Saints!"

"You're not in that, are you, Joey? Then come for a walk to Geisalm, will you?"

"Rather – if Mam'selle says I may. Oh, but you're almost a staff, so that'll be all right," replied Joey, all in a breath.

"Who *is* in the boat?" said Grizel, as she handed her empty cup to Frieda, and lay back in her chair.

"Marie – Frieda – Sophie – Bianca – Anne – Paula – Anita – and Evvy as cox," replied Jo.

"What will the rest do?"

"Bathe, I hope," replied Vanna di Ricci, speaking for the first time since the two old girls had arrived.

"See if you can solve the mystery of the drenched floor, then," advised Jo.

"What's that?" demanded Grizel curiously. "It sounds like the latest detective novel."

"We got permission to bathe this afternoon," explained Jo. "When we got to the bathing-house we found the floor simply floating with water. Someone must have been there; and we know it's not any of us. Must have been some visitor or other."

"What – without asking if they might? What a nerve!" cried Grizel.

"Well, it seems to be the only way we can account for it. Come on an' help to carry the crocks back to the kitchen, you folks. – Frieda, yell for some of those kids to come and help." Jo got up from her seat on the grass, and lifted the huge urn. Simone went to her assistance, and

Frieda obligingly called to some of the Middles to come and help. This was the understanding on which they ever had outdoor meals: they must always clear for themselves. It was only the work of a few minutes, and it saved the servants, who had quite enough to do as it was. When it was done the bathers vanished to get towels and swimming suits, while the crew went off to get into regulation boating kit.

Juliet and Jo got their hats, since the sun was still beating down, and strolled through the gates of the school garden and along the lake-side path towards the Geisalm way. People looked after them as they went. They were known throughout the little peninsula to the residents, and the visitors, who were rapidly growing in number now that the summer had really come, found them a striking contrast. Jo was so dark; Juliet was so fair. Both were tall, though Juliet had the advantage of the younger girl by a couple of inches. Both were slight and graceful. Both were deeply absorbed in themselves. They talked earnestly as they went along and never saw other people.

A certain young man on the veranda of the Kron Prinz Karl looked after them and heaved a deep sigh. If only Juliet hadn't *been* Juliet Carrick! If only Kay, his beloved sister, hadn't been so dead against her when she found out who the girl was! Unaware of his very presence, Juliet went past the hotel, laughing and talking with Jo, and it seemed to the unfortunate young fellow that she did it deliberately. With another deep sigh he went in and got his line, and had himself rowed out to the centre of the lake, where he sat oblivious of the glowing sun and his boatman's bewilderment. For who could expect the fish to bite when that glare was on the waters? Of a certainty the noble Herr must be quite mad!

Meanwhile, Juliet and Jo were going along the narrow path, under the grateful shelter of the pine woods which here stretch down to the edge of the lake. Across the path, beaten hard by the tread of many generations of feet, bright-hued beetles ran, intent on their business; a scarlet-winged butterfly paused on the wing, and then darted off again as the two girls approached him; somewhere overhead a bird was carolling gaily; a faint breeze stirred the short grass, starred with gentian, heartsease and a hundred other flowers. On one bush the alpenroses were glowing with their warm fire. It was a glorious evening and the girls felt its calm as they strolled along, discussing school affairs, and particularly the mystery as to how the bathing-house floor could have been soaked as it had been.

"Well, I give it up," said Juliet finally. "Unless it is, as you say, some visitor who has used the place, I don't see what the explanation can be."

"Well, as it has CHALET SCHOOL BATHING HOUSE stuck up outside, I think whoever it was had a good nerve," said Jo resentfully.

A scrambling near at hand interrupted them, and they looked up in time to see a small girl of ten, clad in a frock of pale blue linen, come tumbling down the bank. Mercifully for her the path broadened to a little triangle just at this point, or she would certainly have rolled into the lake. As it was, Joey fully expected to hear a splash. Luckily a gorse bush stopped her further progress, and she brushed up against it with an ear-splitting yell.

Jo ran to her, asking in German if she were hurt. Juliet followed in time to hear the rich brogue of South Ireland in the reply.

"Sure, miss, 'tis all prickles Oi am – thank ye koindly!"

Joey stared, and Juliet forgot her young ladyhood as she asked, "Where on earth have you come from?"

"From thim woods, av yez plase," was the reply.

"But – what *are* you doing here – an Irish girl?" demanded Juliet.

The child got to her feet – brown little bare feet, with a blister across one toe – and answered with dignity. "Sure 'tis a short visit Oi am payin'. Anny ob-jections, miss?"

"But where is your nurse – or keeper?' asked Jo. "Surely a kid like you isn't allowed to mess about here on her own. The lake is jolly deep hereabouts," she added severely. "If you fell in, you might easily be drowned."

"Drown, is it? An' meself nigh born in the say!" came the answer, accompanied by a contemptuous sniff. "'Tis not drownin' 'ull be the end av Biddy O'Ryan!"

"Well – hadn't you better be getting back to your own people?" asked Juliet, since the last snub had silenced Jo.

"Oi'll be doin' that in me own toime," retorted the small elf, shaking back the loose masses of her wonderful hair, which swirled around her like a black cloud – the hair-ribbons were adorning a couple of bushes further up in the woods – and examining one tanned arm for scratches. Then she suddenly seemed to remember her manners, for she dropped the arm, made a curtsy, and added, "But thank ye koindly for thinkin' of it, all the same." With that she darted past them towards Briesau, and they were left looking after her in silence.

Jo spoke first. "I seem to know that frock," she observed.

"I dare say you do. Hundreds of kiddies must be wearing frocks like that," replied Juliet, laughing.

Jo shook her head. "It's not that kind of know. I mean I know it individually. I've seen it on someone. That mauve embroidery with the touches of amber are jolly familiar, somehow."

"Oh, they turn out those frocks by the dozen," said Juliet. "Never mind that now, Jo. Get up off the grass and come on, if you want us to get to Geisalm and back before *Abendessen*. We must be punctual, you know. A future staff and the head girl can't afford to be late for meals."

"Oh, *blow* being head girl!" groaned Jo, as she got up from the grass and resettled her big white hat. "Come on, then."

They went on, presently coming to what was known

among the Chaletians as the Dripping Rock. This was a ledge, high up on the cliff, whence a tiny stream that ran across the alm dripped down to the path, and so to the lake. It had worn for itself a narrow course through the path, and this the girls jumped lightly, laughing gaily as they did so. Suddenly the laughter froze on Juliet's lips, and Jo, turning to see why, saw Kay Hillis standing in front of them. She had evidently been to Geisalm, and was now returning. She nodded to them in chilly fashion and stood to one side to let them pass. Jo returned the nod with a haughty stare, her lips setting in straight, severe lines. Juliet made no attempt to do anything. The hurt look in her dark eyes went to the younger girl's heart, and she inwardly made up her mind to make Mrs Hillis smart for her treatment of a girl who had done her no harm.

"Rotten snob!" thought Jo viciously, as she walked along in a silence which Juliet did not seem disposed to break. "*I'll* teach her to hurt old Ju as she had done! Her beastly brother, too!"

The thinking in forbidden language relieved her feelings for the moment, and presently she turned to Juliet with a remark upon the glory of the scene, and for the rest of the way they chatted cheerfully together. But Jo had not forgotten; and events were to move with great rapidity.

CHAPTER XVIII

"Please, Jo, may I ask for some more *Brödchen*?"

Jo Bettany turned an amazed face to Evadne Lannis. "*More Brödchen?* Good gracious, Evadne! That's the third lot for your table!"

"I know – but we're all so fearfully hungry," replied Evadne meekly.

"I think you must all be coming down with some unknown disease. I have never met anything like the way you crowd have been eating these past few days! All right; get it if you want it. But this is to be the last lot, remember."

Evadne went off to get the buttered twists of bread, and Jo once more gave herself up to conversation. It had poured with rain all day, and there had been a heavy thunderstorm in the early afternoon. The result was that *Kaffee und Kuchen* had to be taken in the house; and since the floor of the common room had been newly painted the day before, it had meant having it in the *Speisesaal* at the long tables. This was rather a misfortune for the Middles involved in the hiding of Bridget, since it meant that the amount of food through which they managed to get was noticeable. Ordinarily, it wouldn't have mattered, since the food was set there for everyone and everyone helped herself from the same baskets. But having their afternoon meal like this meant that there was only what was put on to their table. And the Middles felt that their suddenly increased appetites had already received enough notice at other meals without this one being added. You can't undertake to provide for a growing child of ten, and then give her the scraps you would offer a cat or a dog. The Middles had discovered this very early during the proceedings, and were sometimes at their wits' ends to know how to bring Biddy the supplies she needed. And Luise had already complained that the stores in her cupboards were vanishing in a most mysterious way. Suspicion had fallen on various people, but, one by one, they had all displayed unshakeable alibis. Luise felt thoroughly upset and annoyed about it all, and that very day had determined to keep a close watch on the kitchen supplies. A chance word, overheard by Ilonka as she went past the kitchen windows, which always stood wide open in the summer, had given the conspirators a hint of what to expect, and caused a gloom to fall on them. Things were quite difficult enough as it was. This would make it ten times worse. Not that it really would have mattered if Bridget had been found; though *they* did not think that. The great joy of the whole affair was its secrecy, and they had made up their minds to keep it secret as long as they could. Bridget had the appetite of a healthy child of ten, and though she was grateful for all they had done for her, there is no denying the fact that she was getting tired of being perpetually in hiding; having to sleep in the draughty games shed; and living on the strangest mixture of foods. Truly, only the stomach of a healthy schoolgirl could have stood the strains she had put on it in the past few days. Her *Mittagessen* had consisted of some sardines, neatly "hooked" by Evadne during the morning break; two rolls; some butter, none the better for having been kept in an empty tin; three pieces of *Torte* saved by the Middles from their own meal, and rather crumbly from being in their pockets; and a large slab of toffee, offered by Cornelia. Breakfast had been much the same thing; and she could look forward to some twists of fancy bread for her *Kaffee und Kuchen*, together with ripe cherries which Maria and Ilonka had brought between them. Elsie had contrived to fill an empty brilliantine bottle with milk, and though the bottle had been washed after a fashion, the milk retained an odd perfume which did not add to its palatability.

The games shed, though better than spending the

night under the stars, was dark and rather gloomy on this wet day, and Biddy had been genuinely frightened by the thunder. They had managed to smuggle out to her a book or two, and a couple of jigsaw puzzles. But Bridget was not fond of reading, and had no idea how to begin on the puzzles. Altogether, she was inclined to think that the Cecilia Home would not be so bad after all. At least she would not be locked up in a dark shed there when it rained and thundered; and she would have something to do. So, while the Middles were devotedly collecting all the food they could for their foundling, that young lady was making a very determined effort to escape from her durance vile.

It was not an easy matter, for the games shed was lit by small square windows set high up in the walls, and those windows were not made to open. Biddy set a stool on top of the lockers that ran along the walls, and climbed up, and took a survey of the land. It was not encouraging. The rain was slanting down in long, silver spears that hid most of the view from sight, and all she could see was the water-sodden playing fields. Besides, she had just discovered that the windows were hermetically sealed, and she was not sure, even if she did break the panes of one, how she would get through it. It was only by stretching up on tiptoe that she was able to see out at all. Bridget got down from her perch and looked round the gloomy shed, tears pricking at the backs of her eyes. "Oh, wirra, wirra! 'Tis safe at home Oi wish Oi was!" she whispered to herself. Then, because she really was a plucky child, she dashed the back of her hand across her eyes, and tried once more to find a way out. There was a rough wooden bench, where the girls sometimes did odd carpentering jobs, and she exerted her strength, and tugged it over to the window. By the time it was there she was breathless and panting, and her frock was soiled and torn in one or two places. Biddy was Irish and happy-go-lucky, however, so she looked at it with equanimity. "Sure, 'twill wash, and 'twill mend," she thought cheerfully.

The bench stood much higher than the tops of the lockers, and when she had got the stool on it she felt sure that she would be able to reach the window safely. What she had not bargained for when she got there was the fact that the wide lockers made it difficult for her to reach it, even though she now had quite a wide view. Still standing precariously on the top of her tower, and holding on to the window-frame with the tips of her fingers, she stared dismally at the pouring rain, and then turning round, sat down on the stool and burst into loud wails.

Kaffee was over at the school, and Jo Bettany, with most of the evening at her disposal, had suddenly remembered that her tennis shoes needed rewhitening. She slipped on a raincoat, found her beret, and ran across to the games shed where the girls kept their tennis shoes. As she neared the place she was startled to hear sobs of bitter grief proceeding from it. "Great cats alive!" she exclaimed aloud. "Am I going mad? Or has one of the Juniors got shut in there?" She hastened her speed, and fitted the key into the lock at the very moment that Elsie, whose turn it was to feed the foundling, was hunting for it with growing dismay because it was not to be found. Jo turned it, opened the door, and walked in. What she saw drew from her the strictly forbidden exclamation, "Great Caesar's ghost!"

The bench was under one of the windows. On top of it was a little three-legged stool; and, perched on the top of that, her long black plaits dangling down, was a blue-frocked small girl whom she seemed to recognize, though the face was hidden in the small brown hands. At any rate, whoever she was, she had no possible business there, and Jo acted promptly. "Come down at once!" she said in stentorian tones.

The child lifted her head with a start and, quite literally, "came down at once". For her sudden movement upset the stool, precariously poised on the narrow bench, and she fell with a wild yell. Jo sprang forward, and caught at her, managing to break the fall a little, though she could not prevent it altogether. The child landed on the floor with a resounding thud, sat up, and stared at her captor, terror evident in her tear-washed blue eyes. Jo knew her at once. "The Irish kid!" she ejaculated. "Well, I'll be gum-swizzled!"

The sound of her voice galvanized Bridget into action. In one movement she was on her feet and making for the door. But Jo was too quick for her. With a spring she caught the short blue skirts in one hand, while with the other she pushed the door shut. Then, hauling her victim along with her, she made for the lockers, sat down, and pulled the child close to her. "What on earth are you doing *here*?" she demanded.

Biddy looked at her with side, frightened eyes. "Sure, miss, Oi'm doin' no harm," she protested.

"But why here?" asked Jo.

"'Twas a shelter Oi wanted, miss. 'Tis the way the rain do be comin' down."

"I dare say. Who let you in?" Jo sounded frankly sceptical.

"The door was open, miss." So it had been – the previous night.

"Rats! It's never been open today!" returned Jo, still holding her captive firmly.

"It has, thin!" retorted Biddy.

"When?"

Biddy was brought up short. She knew that she must not give her friends away if she could help it. But this big girl with the masterful manner and the keen dark eyes was not the sort of person whose questions you could evade, and she obviously meant to have an answer.

"Sure – Oi don't know," faltered the small girl at last.

"Morning – afternoon – a short time ago?" asked Jo impatiently.

Biddy was silent, and Jo was quick to realize that the

affair was beyond her powers. She looked around the shed, and her eye lighted on a blazer left there by Cornelia the day before. Still holding Bridget by the shoulder, she got up and went to fetch it. As she neared it she stumbled over something, which turned out on examination to be a heap of travelling rugs. A mug and a plate gave further secrets away, and the quick-witted Senior guessed that this was the Middles' latest piece of mischief, and the probable explanation of the abnormal appetites some of them had developed during the last few days. She said nothing, however, but picked up the blazer, and told Biddy shortly to put it on. Biddy did as she was told. Then, her shoes forgotten, Jo led her out of the shed, quite forgetting to lock the door, and marched her up to the school.

She took her straight to the study, where Mademoiselle was busy with arrears of letters, tapped at the door, and walked in. Mademoiselle looked up, and her eyes opened when she saw Jo coming in with an untidy small girl who was quite a stranger to her in her charge. "Josephine!" she exclaimed.

"*This*," said Jo calmly, as she deposited Biddy on the rug by the desk, "is the Middles' latest. I found her in the games shed, locked in. There are some rugs there and some crocks. Goodness knows how long this business had been going on, Mademoiselle. I can't get anything out of her, so I thought I'd better bring her straight to you."

It was at this juncture that Elsie, flinging caution and everything else to the winds, went rushing madly over to the games shed, to find the door wide open, and the bird flown. "Crikey!" she gasped, when a hurried search had assured her that Biddy was not there. "Crikey! Someone must have found her out! We're *for* it this time!"

CHAPTER XIX

Whatever Next?

IN THE STUDY BIDDY was doing her best to protect her helpers. She stood sullenly silent while Mademoiselle plied her with questions.

It was Jo, eventually, who loosened her tongue. "All right," she said. "I can guess who is in this, anyway. Corney and Evvy, I suppose, and Elsie and Margia. It's always they who start the mischief in this school. Which of the others was it?"

Bridget looked at her in amazement. "Who tould yez?" she gasped.

"My own common sense," Jo told her crisply. "Come along. Tell us the rest, and save them the trouble."

Thus persuaded, Bridget added the names of Maria and Ilonka, and Jo nodded her head triumphantly. "I *thought* so!"

"And now, my child, you must tell us who you are, and how you come to be here," said Mademoiselle gently. "We must let your father and mother know at once. They will be terribly anxious about you."

"Sure, 'tis the way Oi haven't any," replied Biddy.

"Haven't any? Do you mean, then, that you are *orpheline?*"

The French word was rather too much for Biddy. She suddenly turned to Jo and grabbed her round the waist, burying her head against her. "Me ma's dead, an' me da too," she sobbed. "'Tis alone Oi am!"

Jo hugged her. "Don't cry, kid. You aren't alone while *we're* here. And surely there must be some aunts or something?"

After a little petting they got her soothed, and then the whole story came out, just as it had come to the

Middles. Mademoiselle's kind heart ached as she listened, and Jo tightened her clasp round the little body on her knee. When it was told, Biddy sat silent. Her head was aching with all the crying, and she was tired out. Mademoiselle recognized this.

"She is worn out, Joey," she said in her own language. "Take her to Matron, and ask her to put her to bed in the sanatorium. We will see what we are to do tomorrow." She held out her hand to Biddy, who was watching her doubtfully from beneath her long lashes. "Come and say '*Bonne nuit*', *petite*, and Joey will take you to our good Matron, who will put you to bed, and give you some good coffee and bread."

Biddy looked at her again. Then, reassured by the kind smile, she slipped down from Jo's knee, and came to the lady's side. "Goodnight to yez," she said, "an' may the angels av Hivin have the makin of yer bed!"

Mademoiselle bent and kissed the little face held up to hers, and then signed to Jo to take the child away. "And ask someone to send those children to me, Jo," she directed, as the head girl led her charge out of the room. "I must hear what they have to say about this."

Meeting Anne Seymour, who stared when she met the pair of them, Joey gave her Mademoiselle's message, and then took Biddy up the stairs and into a pleasant room, colour-washed with yellow, where a small, determined looking woman in neat blue uniform sat sewing. She looked up as Jo entered.

"What now, Jo?" she demanded.

"This is Bridget O'Ryan, Matron," said Jo, mischief in her eyes as she watched Matron's face. "Mademoiselle says will you please put her to bed in the san, and give her a good meal."

Matron got to her feet. "Where on earth has she sprung from?"

"The Middles know; they can tell you," said Jo, with a grin.

Matron uttered a sound midway between a sniff and a snort. Then she turned to Biddy. "Well, come along, child. How old are you? – Mercy on us! That frock belonged to Amy Stevens!"

Biddy looked uncomfortable, and rubbed one bare brown foot over the other. Matron took her by a thin little shoulder, and turned her round. "I remember it – it's the one she's grown out of. I suppose Margia gave it to you?"

"Sure then, an' Oi didn't *stale* it!" said Biddy defiantly, suddenly finding her voice.

"Irish as they make 'em!" said Matron cheerfully. "I didn't suppose you did, child. Well, come along, and we'll see what a good hot bath will do for you. You certainly look as though you stood in much need of it!"

This was true. The day in the games shed had not improved Bridget's appearance, and she was muddy about the legs. All the entreaties of the girls had been unavailing to force her into shoes and stockings. Even the wet day had not done it. Now she was black with mud from the playing fields, and her splendid hair was dusty too. With a curt, "You can leave her to me, thank you, Jo," Matron took her off to the bathroom attached to the sanatorium, and proceeded to treat her as if she were one of the babies from Le Petit Chalet, and gave her a thorough bath. The black hair was loosed from its pigtails, and washed too, and when she was clean and comfortable, with her head done up in a towel, and a fresh suit of pyjamas on, Biddy was wrapped up in a woolly, and set down by the stove, which Matron had stoked up, and given a bowl of hot milky coffee, and rolls and butter to eat with it. Then, while she ate, the small energetic lady who overawed her so much set to work, and rubbed the flowing locks dry, afterwards brushing them till Biddy's small head tingled, before she tied them back from her face, and tucked her up in a comfortable little white bed. Matron's bark was worse than her bite, as most of them knew, so the tucking-up was accompanied by a kiss before she withdrew and left the child to fall asleep.

Meanwhile, Mademoiselle had sent for the Middles concerned in this absurd affair, and catechised them severely. "It was very wrong indeed of you," she said sternly. "Think, if this child had had parents who might have been hunting for her, how sad they must have felt. And what right had you to assume such a charge as a little girl, when you are only children yourselves?"

This, to Evadne and Elsie, who were fifteen, and Ilonka who had nearly reached that responsible age, was a grievous insult, and they all three looked very sulky over it. And even when Mademoiselle had finally released them, their woes were not over. Carla von Flügen came to summon them before a prefects' meeting, and Joey Bettany was far more unsparing than the kindly Head in her comments.

"Where you got the nerve from to do such a thing, I can't think! You ought to be ashamed of yourselves. And who gave you permission to steal food for anyone? Oh, yes!" as Cornelia began a violent protest. "It was stealing all right. As for adopting a kid, and thinking *you* could bring her up among you – well, you stand in much need of bringing up yourselves at the moment, whatever you may be like in a few years' time! I never heard of anything so ridiculous in my life! And how long, pray, did you imagine you could keep her as you were doing? What did you think was going to happen when the holidays came?" She paused, and glared at the delinquents.

"We didn't think of hols," muttered Elsie finally.

"No; I don't suppose you did. And you didn't think what a rotten time the poor kid was having on a wet day, shut into that gloomy shed, with nothing to do, either, did you?"

"We gave her books and puzzles!" cried Evadne, stung to answer by this piece of injustice, as she considered it.

"Even so; would *you* like to be stuck in the games shed for a whole day like that?" They wouldn't; and they knew it. They kept silence, and Jo continued. "And even if you had managed to make arrangements for the holidays, what did you propose to do during the winter? You could scarcely keep her where you had her *then*!"

This was another contingency of which they had not thought, and Jo rubbed it well in. Altogether, by the time she had finished with them she had left them all without a leg to stand on in the way of self-defence. It was a sadder and wiser set of Middles that went upstairs to bed that night, though Jo would have been better advised to restrain her tongue a little.

When she had finished with them, she dismissed them, and then turned to her fellow prefects. "What are we going to do about it?" she asked.

There was a silence, and she went on: "Those wretched children have certainly saddled us with this kid. We can't just send her off to that Home affair after they have taken her up like this. It would be too jolly unfair. So – what are we going to do about it?"

"We had better do as they wished, and adopt her," suggested Marie.

"All very well. Where are we going to get the money from?"

"We keep three beds going in the free ward for children at the Sonnalpe," said Frieda. "Can we not manage to keep this child as well?"

"How?"

"We could – have a Sale of Work, perhaps?" asked Simone doubtfully.

"We might; but it wouldn't go very far, you know. She needs clothes, and food, and a home of some sort, and education – oh, lots of things I could mention. And they all cost money."

The prefects looked at each other.

"What does Mademoiselle say?" asked Frieda.

"That we must think things out for ourselves. She is going to write to the priest at Hall, and this chauffeur's sister, and find out exactly how much of the kid's story is true. If it's quite correct, and she really has no one to look after her, then I suppose it's either the Cecilia Home or us – and there's no doubt about which she'd prefer."

"It must be *us*!" said Marie firmly.

"All very well, but how are we going to do it?"

"We can manage to clothe her amongst us, I suppose," said Carla slowly.

"If we all give so much of our pocket-money we can buy materials, and we can make her garments between us."

"Where will she live?" asked Simone.

"Mademoiselle will settle that," said Vanna di Ricci, speaking for the first time. "Perhaps Madame would let her go up to the Sonnalpe. She would be company for the Robin."

"She'd have to get rid of a good deal of her brogue, then," said Jo, with the first grin they had seen since the affair had come to light. "My sister would never hear of the Robin learning Irish-English."

"Possibly she could do that if she were with people who did not use it," said Simone.

"It's pretty strongly rooted, I should say."

"She would be with Stacie," declared Bianca di Ferrara. "She would soon learn to speak very good English then."

Jo chuckled. "Stacie is learning to speak more like a Christian, and less like a middle-aged professor," she said. "Still, I don't doubt she'd be able to make *some* difference!"

Vanna spoke up again. "It would be a good idea, I think, to have her trained to be maid to the Robin," she said.

Jo stared at her. "My good girl, who's going to pay? Uncle Ted hasn't all that much money – little more than his salary, I believe."

"But if we educated Bridget, and looked after her till she was grown up, would she not be willing from gratitude to serve the Robin?"

"Vanna, you've been reading toshy novels!" accused Jo. "Don't be an idiot, my lamb! That sort of thing is all very well in a book, but it doesn't happen very often in real life – if at all. No; we must think of something better than that. All the same," she went on thoughtfully, "to have her trained as a maid is rather an idea. Her mother seems to have been one to this Miss Honora, and the kid should know something about it. If we could hang on to her till she's fifteen, and then have her taught hairdressing, and so on, it might be the very ticket for her."

"But – how a ticket?" demanded Carla, to whom Jo's slang was at times incomprehensible.

Jo looked ashamed of herself. "I mean – just the thing for her," she amended hurriedly.

"Then we must decide what we shall do about paying for her," said Frieda, "and I have an idea for that."

"What is it? Let's have it," said Jo.

"Let us do it as *Guides*."

There was a little pause, as they looked appreciatively at each other. This was a brilliant idea. As a school they had quite enough charities to see to, as Jo remarked. But as Guides, they could use some of the Guide funds which had been steadily accumulating during the three years they had had the Company. Also, it was more than likely that the Guides of the other school at Buchau, St Scholastika's, would want to join in, too. To make it a Guide concern would solve a good many difficulties.

"That's a splendid idea, Frieda!" said Jo enthusiastically. "I vote we act on it at once. We'll just draw up some sort of note about it, and show it to Mademoiselle. She will tell my sister, and we must ask Bill and the rest of the officers what they think. They'll be almost certain to agree; and we can do it. Frieda! You're a genius!"

Quiet Frieda blushed rosy-red at this enconium, and

the rest thronged round her to congratulate her and pat her on the back. At length she contrived to break away from them. "I think you are all very silly!" she cried in her own language. "As for you, Jo, I wish you would try to grow up! You are so very head girl sometimes; and then you behave like a Junior – like this, for instance! Oh, go away, and let me alone! If I hadn't thought of it, someone else would!"

They let her alone after that; but for the rest of the evening they were engaged in drawing up a written account of their scheme, and when Jo went along to the study to say *Gute Nacht*, she solemnly presented one copy to Mademoiselle; another to the Guide officers who were taking coffee with the Head; and posted a third and fourth to the Sonnalpe and St Scholastika's respectively the next morning.

The idea recommended itself to the authorities; and at the end of a week it was all arranged. Bridget was to live over at Le Petit Chalet. She would go to the little school up at St Scholastika village at the other end of the lake; and the Guides were to be entirely responsible for her keep and clothing – both Companies.

CHAPTER XX

The Boat Race

ONCE BRIDGET WAS SAFELY SETTLED up at the school, with the two Guide Companies responsible for her welfare, the girls turned to work and play with increased vim. Term was nearly over – there was not a month left, and a good deal had to be crammed into the time.

The most important of all, from their point of view, was the boat race between the two schools. Hitherto, the Chalet had sighed for worlds to conquer. With the arrival of St Scholastika's those worlds had arrived. Tennis, hockey, cricket and netball had all been played between the two little communities. The Chalet had beaten St Scholastika at cricket and hockey, and been beaten at netball. The finals of the tennis were still to be played off. Only those and the boat race remained to be decided.

Both schools were excellent, for St Scholastika's had always been accustomed to river work, and two summers before, Mrs Russell had presented her own school with racing-skiffs, and bidden them go ahead. Living beside a lake, it was natural that all should be keen, and the thought of some day being in the boat had persuaded a good many nervous people to overcome their fears and learn to swim and dive.

The girls would have liked to make a regular regatta of it, but there was no means of doing so. Neither school had a private swimming-pool, and the Heads of both had no idea of allowing their girls to give a public display. But boat-racing was another matter. Therefore, both teams had worked early and late; they had followed the latest dietary systems, and on the Saturday afternoon after the discovery of Biddy and the Middles' latest iniquity, they marched down to the boat-house in fine fettle. News of the forthcoming race had got about among the visitors, and the girls found that they had a goodly number of spectators to face.

The course, which had been taped out earlier in the day by some of the doctors from the Sonnalpe, Herr Braun of the Kron Prinz Karl, and the old priest who served the various chapels round the lake, lay between Briesau and Seehof, on the other side. This made a course nearly a mile and a half in length – "quite enough for girls to attempt," declared Dr Jem and Dr Jack

Maynard. Dr Gottfried Mensch was to act as starter, and Herr Braun and Vater Ambrosius would be the judges. The judges' boat was already comfortably established at the other side, with the two judges and various members from the staffs of both schools sitting waiting.

The Saints were there already, looking rather nervous as they came forward to greet their opponents. Marie, as captain of the boat, held out her hand to Gipsy Carson of St Scholastika's – a slim, dark girl whose prettiness, striking though it was, faded to mere commonplace beside Marie's exceptional beauty.

"You're early," said the latter.

"The Fawn was agitating till we got off," explained Gipsy. "She goes on like a scared hen trying to cross the road between two motors, sometimes! This was one."

Marie laughed at the irreverent description, and the two captains walked down to the slipway together. Boating-kit for the schools consisted of knee-length loose knickers, covered by jumper-tunics, all in white. Narrow bands of gold and brown on the Chalet tunics distinguished them from the Saints, whose bands were of saxe-blue. All wore white hats, for the heat of the sun was great this month, and the school bands encircled the crowns. Bare of legs, with rope-soled sandals, their jumpers sleeveless and loose, they looked fit and ready for the fray. People with long hair had twisted it round their heads to keep it out of the way; and Evadne's short curls were snooded to keep them out of her eyes. At various points down the course the big, steady tubs generally used on the lake were stationed, with throngs of excited girls in them. The two little steamers were anchored at various places of vantage, and were packed with visitors and people from the summer chalets round. One or two privately-owned motor-boats were there too, and the banks of the lake near the starting- and the winning-posts were black with people.

"What awful crowds!" muttered Gipsy anxiously, as

she separated from Marie. "I hope to goodness it doesn't send some of those idiots off their heads and lose us the race!"

"*I* hope there aren't any accidents," said pretty Anne Seymour, who was following them. "It's a good thing all our crowd can swim."

Gipsy nodded. "Not all ours can, so they are stuck pretty near the bank over there," she said. "Time, is it? Come on, then, you people."

The crews parted and got to their own boats. Marie, at stroke, turned and glanced back at her crew. "Listen for Evvy," she said.

They nodded, and then there was silence. Gipsy could be heard giving the same instructions to her men as she settled down and took her oar. Marc Strauss and Hansel Laneck, two of the oldest boatmen on the lake, proceeded to push the boats off, and the girls paddled up to the starting point, where the tape was held by Miss Nalder of the Chalet and Miss Harris of St Scholastika's. This was responsible work for the two little coxes – Evadne Lannis and Winnie Silksworth. However, they had both had plenty of practice in the art, and the boats took station without much trouble.

There was an almost breathless silence as they waited for the sound of the starting gun, and the two crews stared ahead nervously, not seeing anything clearly. Just as Marie was beginning to feel that she must shriek if they didn't get off, the first shot sounded. They laid firm hold of their oars; the coxes held their rudder lines in their left hands ready to drop the holding chain with the right. – *Bang!* The second shot resounded over the silent lake, and the two tape-holders dropped the tape more loosely. *Bang!* And they were off.

A mile and a half is not a heavy distance for men to row; but is is a pretty heavy test for schoolgirls. Marie knew that she must not spurt too soon, or they would be lost. Keeping her crew at a steady twenty-eight to the minute, she worked steadily, setting a beautiful example in serenity of demeanour, whatever she might be feeling inside. Gipsy was no whit behind her. The Saints were slightly ahead, having got off a shade more promptly than the Chaletians, but it was not half a length. Some of the more inexperienced members of the Chalet School saw this advantage with dismay; however, they were forced to keep quiet, since there was a prefect to every boat from each school, and any outcry would have been summarily dealt with once the race was over. For the same reason, small Saints were unable to gloat aloud. But both sets might – and *did*! – cheer their own men, and such a pandemonium was surely never heard on the lake before. The visitors listened to the noise indulgently, while the schools yelled at the full pitch of healthy lungs: "Now then, Chalet!" – "Come on, Saints!" – "Pitch in, Marie!" – "Go it, Gipsy!" – and the like. When the boats had gone halfway down the course the Saints were still leading, though both crews had quickened a little. This was the undoing of the Saints. Suddenly convinced that they were the superior, and longing for a spectacular finish, Gipsy quickened her stroke too soon, and drew away from the Chalet boat. Marie managed to keep her feelings under control and plugged steadily on. Evadne, an excellent cox, looked ahead. "They're tiring!" she yelled – and even so, the crew scarcely heard her above the yells of the spectators. "Now then – make it!"

It was broiling hot. Marie was damp with perspiration, and her breath was coming quickly already. Her arms felt stiff, and her legs were no better. But she knew that the Saints must be in the same case. A quarter of the way from home she looked at Evadne, and gasped, "Going to – spurt!"

Evadne, clinging to her rudder lines, and dexterously steering so that the boat got as little of the Saint's backwash as possible, caught the words. Opening her mouth, she bettered her former yell. "Get ready to spurt!" she bawled.

Again the crew heard her, and set themselves to this final effort. Evadne watched Marie's face intently. She saw the word "Spurt!" formed by the elder girl's lips, and responded at once. With a howl that any skipper bawling from the bridge during a gale might have envied, she flung the word along the boat, and the crew heard. They responded with the last ounce that was in them. The boat simply cut through the water. In vain Gipsy tried to rouse her own wearied men to beat them. She had begun too soon, and they could not give her any more. The Chalet boat levelled with the Saints; they drew past; they had the advantage. The Saints, all out by this time, wallowed helplessly in their backwash. A yell of triumph went up as the Chaletians cut over the place where the tape had been stretched, winners by a length and a half.

The crew themselves were all in. They lay over their stretchers, panting, exhausted, and dead to their victory for the moment. Eager people rushed to help them, and presently they were standing on the bank, where they were escorted to one of two tents set up for the occasion; there they were rubbed down by admirers, dosed with milk and soda, and helped into fresh clothes. When they finally emerged, themselves again, they found that the Saints had had to submit to the same thing. However, it was all very refreshing, and Marie, whose second wind had come back by this time, even felt that she wouldn't have minded rowing back to the school.

Then she heard her name called, and turned to see Gipsy coming to her with outstretched hand. "Splendid race, Marie, old girl! You people are jolly good!"

"It took us all we knew to beat you," responded Marie. "I was done when we reached the winning-place."

"So were we!" laughed Gipsy. "Come along and be congratulated by the Heads and the staffs."

Marie would rather have been spared this, but there

was no getting out of it, and she went through it with a charming grace, which drew many admiring eyes to her. When, later, the big silver cup presented for the race by the King of Belsornia was handed to her by the local lord of the manor, the Baron von und zu Wertheimer, he noticed her keenly. A very charming romance for little Marie resulted from that presentation in the coming years; but that, as Kipling says, is another story. At present, it is sufficient to say that the Baron, who was a pleasant young man of twenty-two, who had been educated at Oxford, expressed his great pleasure in giving the cup to the Chalet School; and then, as soon as he decently could, took off the Chalet captain of the boat to the big marquee erected outside the Hotel Seehof, and treated her to ices and lemonade ad lib.

Altogether, it was a very jolly day, as Joey remarked later on, when the Juniors and the Middles had gone to bed, and the Seniors were indulging in a last stroll before following their example.

CHAPTER XXI

Donal

PERHAPS IT WAS THE EXCITEMENT of the school winning the boat race. Perhaps it was, as Jem said later, natural depravity. The fact remains that Joey Bettany took matters into her own hands, and the course of Juliet's life was changed thereby.

It all began with a stroll the head girl took on the Sunday afternoon following that exciting Saturday.

Most of the girls were resting, but Joey, feeling restless, went to Miss Wilson, the mistress on duty, and got permission to take a walk instead. "I'm so revved up," she explained to the mistress, "I simply *can't* rest. Please, may I go for a walk instead?"

Miss Wilson looked at her sharply. All her life Jo's restless temperament was to give her trouble. On such an occasion as this, the authorities had long recognized that exercise was the best for her. If she were forced to rest now, she would probably spend half the night tossing about, and that was a thing to be avoided at all costs. So "Bill", wise in her generation, merely said, "Well, don't go beyond the peninsula, and either wear a hat or take a sunshade."

Jo pulled a face once her back was turned, but she had got what she wanted, so she thought it wiser to abstain from comment, and went out meekly to seek one of the big Japanese sunshades which were much in vogue with the girls this term. Presently "Bill", from her deck-chair near the roses, saw her setting forth bearing a scarlet monstrosity which was known to the school as "The Red Peril". It suited Jo, however, and looked well with her white frock and black head. "Bill" smiled to herself, and then returned to her magazine, and thought no more about it.

It was a hot Sunday, and the girls, especially those who had helped to win the boat race, were nearly all slumbering peacefully. Simone Lecoutier, it is true, was reading, and lifted her head long enough to send a reproachful glance after her chum; but Jo did not see it, so was unaffected by it. In one of several hammocks slung between the trees Juliet Carrick was fast asleep; Grizel Cochrane, Frieda Mensch, and Marie von Eschenau were all writing letters, with frequent intervals for gossip and chocolate. Therefore none went with Jo, and she was able to wreak her will without any detaining force.

Once she had left the fields, she turned towards the grateful shade of the pine trees that grow up the slopes of the Bärenbad Alpe, and was presently among them. There, she put down her sunshade, and walked slowly along, her eyes on the ground, her thoughts busy with Juliet, Mrs Hillis, and Mr O'Hara.

"I should like to wring that woman's neck!" she thought. "How dare she treat Juliet like that? It doesn't matter what her father was – he was pretty rotten, I dare say – look at the way he dropped Ju on to Madge all those years ago! – but that doesn't say that *she* is a beast. I'll bet there were some pretty rotten O'Haras a generation or two back if they chose to look!"

By this time she had arrived at the foot of the path that led up to the *Gasthaus* where the girls often went to have saucers of cream and wild strawberries. It was too hot even for this climb, however, so she turned aside, and went along a narrow byway that led, as she knew, to a point from which it was possible to get a glorious view of the lake. So intent was Jo on her thoughts that she never looked where she was going. Consequently she did not see the figure of a young man stretched out near a log, and tripped over his outstretched feet.

To fall headlong over a perfect stranger would have been upsetting enough. But when she had got to her feet again, and was beginning to stammer out apologies, she made the pleasing discovery that it was no other than Donal O'Hara himself who was standing before her, a worried look on his face, for Jo had gone with a crash.

"I am most awfully sorry—" he was beginning. Then he stopped. The schoolgirl to whom he had begun his speech had suddenly changed into a young fury with flashing black eyes and scarlet cheeks, and the change was so startling that he was silenced by it.

"*You!*" said Jo, icy contempt in her voice.

"Yes," he said meekly. "'Tis me, Miss Jo."

"My name's Bettany," returned Jo curtly.

"I – I beg your pardon, Miss Bettany."

"Thank you!" flashed Jo.

He stared at her, wondering for a moment if the heat of the sun had affected her. "It's very hot," he ventured.

"I hope you'll end up in a hotter place than this!" retorted Jo – most inexcusably.

"Why, Miss – er – Bettany—" he began. But he was not allowed to finish.

With a fine sweep, Jo turned her back on him, and began to walk rapidly away. As she did so she dropped her handkerchief, and what could the wretched youth do but pick it up and go after her with it?

"I say! Miss Bettany – Miss Bettany!" he shouted.

The only answer Jo made was to quicken her pace. All his natural perversity aroused, young O'Hara promptly began to run. At that, Jo stopped dead, and turned to face him.

"Will you kindly stop chasing me?" she demanded furiously.

"But, hang it all—" he was beginning in aggrieved tones, when she interrupted him.

"That will do, thank you. Go away; I don't want to see you again."

"Why not?" he asked, his Irish temper suddenly roused by this last piece of rudeness. And, indeed, Jo's behaviour was quite indefensible.

"Because I consider you an utter cad!" was the soothing reply.

He glared at her. "And you are an impertinent school-girl, miss!"

Jo was scarlet with rage already, so she couldn't go red; but she could, and did, meet his angry eyes with a fury that startled him.

"Your opinion doesn't weigh very much with me, I'm afraid," she said curtly. "And now, if that's all you've got to say, please go away, and leave me alone. You might have saved yourself your run at this rate."

For reply, he flung her handkerchief at her feet. "An' there's the reason for my trouble!" he cried. "'Twill be the long time, I'm thinking, before I'll bother me head to do anything for anyone again!"

Jo looked at the handkerchief. Then she stooped and picked it up. "I beg your pardon," she said quietly. "I didn't know I'd lost it. Thank you for bringing it to me."

The anger had faded out of her eyes for the moment, and she looked more like the jolly schoolgirl of whom his sister had spoken before that fatal day when they had met her with Juliet Carrick. The memory made his own anger cool, and he smiled at the girl.

Now, Donal O'Hara had one of the most charming smiles in the world. His mother had always declared it must have been a christening gift from some fairy. As a little boy, he had only had to turn it on and very few people had been able to resist it. It partly accomplished its usual work at that moment, and Jo sat down on a near-by log and mopped her hot face with the handkerchief he had returned to her so rudely. The sight of it brought back his own behaviour, and he flushed. "I apologize for being so rude to you," he said. "Sure, I ought to be kicked for treating a lady like that."

Jo had a charming smile of her own, and she turned it on to him. "I deserved it," she admitted frankly.

He came down, and sat on the grass at her feet. "Miss Jo," he said, "what have I done that you should hate me so?"

The smile faded, and Jo's face darkened. "If you look back, you'll soon see," she said.

He looked at her. "You mean – Miss Carrick?" he asked.

Jo's anger blazed up again at the mention of Juliet's name. "I think you ought to be ashamed of yourself!" she said hotly. "To behave to any girl as you did is iniquitous!"

"It – it – is so hard to explain," he said.

"I can believe that," replied Jo dryly.

"No; you can't. I don't mean to be rude, Miss Joey; but, after all, 'tis only a schoolgirl you are. What can you know about it?"

Jo looked at him. "I'm almost seventeen," she said conveniently ignoring the fact that she was a good four months off that age. "Here we grow up pretty quickly, you know. Most of our girls who are married are only two or three years older than I. And I *do* know that to let a girl be your pal, and then to turn against her because your sister told you that her father wasn't all you could ask is the act of a cad and – and – a bounder!"

Young O'Hara flushed. "Maybe 'twasn't that intirely. Maybe 'twas the old name we're all so proud of—"

"*You're* a credit to it, aren't you?" asked Jo cruelly.

She got home there. Donal O'Hara was *not* proud of the way he had behaved to the girl who had been his sister's friend. Perhaps, all unknown to either of them, Kay's influence had been lessened by her marriage. At any rate, he lifted his head, and looked Jo in the eyes. "Ye know I am not," he said simply.

His honesty softened Jo. "Then – why don't you be?" she asked with a simplicity that matched his own.

He looked at her. "Ye mean—"

Jo threw caution and discretion to the winds. "Why don't you ask Juliet about things yourself? Listen, Donal! Juliet's father was all you may have heard of him – and more! D'you know what they did to poor Ju? Taught her to think that she was nothing but a nuisance, and tried to unload her on to my sister. It was only when he was dying that he even attempted to make up to her for the way they treated her. How do you think she must feel about the way Kay and you chucked her when you heard about her people? And she's been badly hurt already, without that added."

Donal squatted on the log, and pulled her down beside him. "'Tis hot the sun is," he remarked. "Put up that thing" – pointing to the scarlet sunshade – "and tell me all about it."

Thus encouraged, Joey did as he asked and, by the end of an hour, during which she had nearly talked herself hoarse, he knew all there was to know about Juliet's pitiful past. And as they talked, the last remnants of the schoolboy who had been influenced by a sister fell away from him, and he sat up a man.

"Thank you, Joey," he said, when she had finished. "I'll not be forgetting what I owe ye for this – not ever. If I can help you at any time, ye may depend on me. An' now, we'll be fixing things, for Juliet is angry with me, and a good right she has!"

"How do you mean – fixing things?" asked Jo doubtfully.

"Would she be seeing me if I was to walk up to the door and ring the bell, and ask for her? Ye know she would *not*. Well, then, 'tis you will have to help me, the way she'll not be able to help herself."

Jo sat back and gasped. "Me help you to take Juliet away from us?" she cried with more fervency than grammar. "Don't be an idiot! As if I should!"

Donal looked at her with that smile of his. "Ye'll not be refusing when 'tis for her happiness," he urged softly.

Jo's head fell, and she looked crestfallen. "But – is it?" she argued.

"Isn't it? Ah, Joey, *mo chuisla*, wasn't it yourself that told me she was hurt? Won't you be giving me the chance to mend that hurt?"

There was a silence. Then Jo turned to him. "All right," she said. "I'll help you if I can – I mayn't be able to, of course," she added, as an afterthought.

"You will, though," he said, confidence in his tone.

Joey sighed. "Well – there won't be any service tonight. We'll all go for a walk instead. I'll get Juliet and Frieda and Marie and Simone—"

"I say, you needn't be bringing the whole school!" he interrupted, dismay in his tones.

"Don't be silly!" snapped Jo. "We're at school! We can't just go off by ourselves when we like! What I was going to say is that I'll bring them, and we'll all come up here. I'll be tired, and sit down here, and get Ju to stay with me while the others go on. Then, I'll make an excuse to leave her for a moment – and that's where *you* enter. I can't do any more. You'll have your chance, anyway."

She consoled herself with the thought that it was in the highest degree unlikely that Juliet would even agree to listen to anything he might have to say, and having arranged the time with him, went back to school, and managed to get her party together. All went according to plan. Juliet was easily persuaded to sit down and chat with Jo while the others went on further up the path. It is true there was a little difficulty with Simone; but Joey got rid of her finally. For a few minutes the two girls had the place to themselves. Then Jo's quick ear caught the sound of footsteps, and with a murmur about her stocking coming down, she fled to the bushes, just as Donal came round the bend in the road.

What happened after that nobody ever knew, for neither of the principal actors would ever tell. But it is a fact that the Juliet who had gone out with tragedy in her dark eyes had vanished by the time the schoolgirls, headed by Jo and Simone, arm-in-arm, appeared on the scene, and the old Juliet, dimpling and blushing, had come back. Also, on the Monday evening, after spending a day in Innsbruck, the pair returned, looking extra pleased with themselves, and Joey, before she went to bed that night, was shown a ruby-and-diamond ring on her friend's left hand which made her exclaim with pleasure at the beauty of the stones even before she said mournfully, "Another one gone! Oh, isn't growing up *horrid*?"

CHAPTER XXII

The Sonnalpe Again

"Has it been a good term, Joey?"

"I don't – know."

"Do not know?" Gisela Mensch raised her delicately-marked brows at Jo and dropped her sewing into her lap.

They were sitting in the garden of Die Rosen, with the roses that gave the chalet its name in full bloom all round them. Term had ended the day before, and Joey had been at the Sonnalpe since the early morning. Juliet had gone to Ireland with the Hillises and Donal, to meet his father and mother, and see where her future home would be. The wedding would not take place for three years yet, for both were very young, and Donal was still at Oxford. So Juliet would come back in September and be Head at the Chalet annexe at the Sonnalpe, where they would begin with twenty-two girls. Until Donal was ready she would be there, and when she went they hoped that Simone would come out to take up her post. Joey was jubilant about this, though she looked at the future with melancholy eyes when she thought of the thousands of miles that would separate her and Juliet, for Donal was to read for the Bar, and the pair must, of necessity, live in London. Sir Murtagh O'Hara had promised that he would allow the young pair enough for them to live on till Donal could make a living at his profession. Juliet had a little through the sale of her mother's jewels, and Jem, by means of careful invest-ment, had already doubled it for her. Jo knew all this, and it troubled her when she thought of it.

Wanda was at the Sonnalpe, too, with her tiny son; pretty Bette Rincini, one of the first of the Chalet girls, was betrothed, and would be wedded the next spring; and Gertrud Steinbrücke, another of the old girls, was looking very pretty and shy, and a certain young doctor who had recently come to join at the sanatorium the band of those who help to fight the white plague, spent a good deal of his spare time with her. And Jo herself would be seventeen the next term. It was all very upsetting, and Jo hated it, though not so badly as she had done four months before. Now, as Gisela looked at her, she rolled over on the grass where she was lying, and tipped her straw hat further over her face.

"In some ways, I suppose it has been a jolly good term. We've won the cricket match and the boat race. And if we *did* lose the tennis, we didn't disgrace ourselves, anyhow. The weekend camps were topping, and the Saints have made a jolly good beginning as Guides. Yes; it hasn't been bad, on the whole."

Wanda looked up from her little Kurt, who was lying in her lap, staring solemnly at the roses behind his mother. "I think it has been very good, Joey, *mein Liebling*. And Juliet is happy again, and that was *your* doing, for she says so."

Joey laughed. "It may have been the shock my rudeness gave him – I was as rude as I knew how," she added frankly.

"Whatever it was, it has given Juliet her happiness. You will always be glad to think that, Joey."

Grizel appeared at this moment, bearing a tray with glasses and a brimming jug on it. "Who speaks for drinks?" she cried.

"Me!" said Jo, rolling over once more, and sitting up. "Grizelda, you really are a peach!"

Grizel set down her burden on the grass, and proceeded to fill the glasses and hand them round. "Sort of strawberryade," she said explanatorily. "I got the recipe from Giulia Bernadetti, one of the people at the Conservatoire. Jolly good too."

"It *is*," said Joey appreciatively, as she drained her glass.

"What were you people talking about?" asked Grizel, as she squatted down beside her.

"School, and the kind of term it's been," said Jo. "Any more of that stuff, Grizel? Thanks! It's nectar – and not too sweet, either."

"Leave some for Madame," Grizel warned her. "The lot is there."

"*And* the kids," added Jo. "Isn't the Robin coming on now?"

"It is so good to think that there is little need to fear for her," said Gisela softly. "They say, Joey, that she will be stronger than she has ever been after this year."

"She has grown," put in Wanda. "And how pretty she is!"

"Here they come!" And Grizel jumped to her feet to set up a deck-chair for Madge, who came across the lawn propelling Stacie's wheelchair, while Stacie herself held Master David on her knee. With them were the Bettany twins and the Robin, whose baby chubbiness was completely gone now, though she showed the same black curls and rosy face and deep eyes. Her bare legs were tanned and scratched, for she had been gathering *Blaubeeren* the day before, and her arms were in even worse condition. As for the twins, they were brown and sturdy, and as much of imps as always.

Only Madge herself showed little change. She was as slim and girlish-looking as she had been when she came out to the Tyrol, five years before, to open the Chalet School. There was a tender look in her deep brown eyes, and her smile was even sweeter than it had been then. But she looked no older, for all her cares and responsibilities. She sat down now with a smile, when she had manoeuvred Stacie's chair into a shady spot, and accepted the glassful of pink drink that Grizel brought her. Jo took her small nephew from Stacie, and set him down on the grass to play at his heart's content. The Robin dropped down beside her beloved Jo, and there was silence for a little space.

"Where's Biddy?" asked Jo idly, after a pause.

"Gone to help with the milking," replied Madge, setting down her glass. "Jo, there's a letter from Juliet come for you. I see the postmark is Ireland, so they must have got to Carrickglas safely. No; I didn't bring it – it's in your bedroom, with some other letters that came."

Jo was on her feet and off to the house in an instant.

"I wonder what they think of Juliet, now they have her?" mused Grizel.

"Oh, but they must love her, of course," said Gisela quickly. "Our dear Juliet! She was one of the best head girls we ever had!"

"A long way better than me," Grizel frowned to herself.

Madge shook her curly head with a smile, "Nonsense, Grizel! You were an excellent head girl – I could not have asked for a better, as I told you this time last year. And now that you are to make your home with us, and help up here at the annexe, I am more pleased than I can say."

Grizel flushed, and her grey eyes filled suddenly with tears. "It – it was your doing, Madame," she stammered. "I don't think anyone else would have had the patience with me that you had. Even that last mad trick of mine you forgave, and gave me another chance. I'd have been a cad if I hadn't played up after that!"

"What was that?" asked Gisela curiously.

"Something that we have all agreed to forget," said Madge quickly. "Here comes Jo with her letters."

Jo came tearing back across the grass, with no heed for the heat of the day, and her sister laughed as she plumped down.

"Afraid you'll catch cold if you don't keep moving?" teased Grizel.

"Don't be an ass!" retorted Jo. "Madge! It's all OK!

They love Juliet already, and she's having a great time. And there's a letter from Elisaveta, and she says that if I can't go to her, she must come here."

"Cheers!" cried Grizel. "Won't it be fun to see Veta again! What else does she say, Jo?"

Jo was scanning the sheets rapidly. "Says she is coming to the Sonnalpe next week for a month. She's been working hard, and the doctors think she needs a complete rest. She says: 'Won't it be fun? We'll go bare-foot again, and dash about as we used to when I was at school. I'm not even having a lady-in-waiting with me this time. Madame will look after me. Of course, there'll be the usual fuss when I'm coming; but they'll all go back, once they've seen me safely into her hands.' I *say*! What a gorgeous joke! She's going to forget she's a princess, and I shall jolly well forget I'm a head girl!"

The Robin, who had become interested in the conversation when she heard the name of the young Crown Princess of Belsornia, wriggled over to Jo and tumbled into her lap. "Don't you like being head girl now, Joey?" she asked.

"Sometimes," replied Jo, with an arm round her. "It's quite fun at times; but there are lots of others when I wish the wretched post had never been invented."

"I wish I could come back to the Chalet," sighed the small girl. "I do so want to see you as head girl, and now I shall not."

"Well, you're not missing much," Jo assured her, with an infectious grin.

"Besides, you are going to be a prefect here at the annexe, Robin," put in Madge. "Signa and you and Amy will have any amount to do."

"She's *not*!" cried Jo incredulously. "Why, what age will the kids be up here?"

"All under twelve at present," replied her sister. "And Robin will be one of our oldest girls, and has grown up under the prefect system. Stacie" – she smiled at the other girl as she spoke – "knows very little about it, and will not be in school for long just yet; though we hope that when the Easter term begins she will be able to be like the others. But the doctors say we must make haste slowly, and she will only have a couple of hours in the morning, and an hour in the afternoon, for the present. And the other two people who are coming, and who are older than our three, are two little French girls who have never been to school in their lives, and know nothing about it. Robin and Amy and Signa will manage very well, I know."

"And will you help with the teaching?" asked Grizel.

Madge nodded. "At first, at any rate. Davie is not in any need of me during the mornings, nowadays. Later – well, we'll leave 'later' to look after itself. But, for this first term, I shall teach in the mornings."

"It's not fair!" cried Jo rebelliously. "If you're going to teach, Madge, I think you ought to come to *us*!"

Madge laughed. "Joey, darling, how could I? I can teach here all right, where I am on the spot. But what would happen to things if I came down to Briesau for the term?"

"They'd get on all right," grumbled Jo. "Marie does most of the housekeeping now, anyway."

"Marie will be busy this winter. No; ask no questions, Joey, for I shan't answer them. It's *her* secret – not mine. Tell us who the rest of your letters are from."

Jo looked at her letters. "From Frieda, and Bernie. I'll read them, shall I, and tell you the news?"

They agreed, and Jo ripped her letters open and skimmed the contents. "Bernie and Kurt are coming to Innsbruck for Christmas!" she said, when she had finished. "Isn't that splendid?"

Wanda, who had been playing with her son, looked up. "But did I not tell you?" she queried. "I knew that two days ago."

"Wanda, you pig!" cried Jo. "No; you never told us!"

"You don't deserve it," said Madge severely. "What language, Jo!"

Jo cast an appealing glance at her. "It's out of term, Madge."

"Doesn't make any difference – with babies like Peggy and Rix to hear you and copy you. You might try to remember that you're an *aunt*, Joey, even if you do try to forget that you're a head girl during term."

"How I loathe growing up!"

Madge laughed, and went to rescue her son, who had fallen flat on his face in a flower-bed, and was voicing his woes for all to hear.

By degrees, the little group split up. Wanda went to lay Baby Kurt in his cradle, and Gisela took her tiny daughter home, as she was expecting some friends for *Kaffee und Kuchen*. Grizel wandered off by herself, and Madge escorted the three small ones indoors to get ready for tea. Only Stacie and the Robin were left with Jo.

"Do you *really* not like being head girl, Joey darling?" asked the Robin.

Jo laughed. "I told you, *Herzliebchen*. Sometimes I do, and sometimes I don't."

The Robin sat silent.

"I think you are very lucky, Jo," said Stacie presently.

"Oh?" Jo looked at her curiously. "Why do you think that?"

The younger girl flushed a little, but she answered, "All the girls look up to you, and follow you. You can do a tremendous lot with them if you like, because you are head girl, as well as because they like you so much. It's a tremendous thing, really."

"I know," said Joey.

The Robin spoke her thoughts aloud. "I hope Amy and Signa and me will be able to be as good prefects as the Chalet School ones. It will be very difficult, though."

"You'll manage," said Stacie briefly.

Jo turned her face towards the mountains on the other side of the lake. A soft flush was in her cheeks, and her eyes were full of dreams.

"What are you thinking, Jo?" asked the Robin.

"Thinking of this term." Jo looked away for another minute. Then she turned to the other two. "In one way, you know, I'm fearfully proud of being head girl; and – I suppose – all that about being fed up with it isn't really true. I – I *do* like it, now I'm accustomed to it... Listen! There's the bell for *Kaffee*! Come on, Robin! – Stacie, take her on the chair, and I'll give you both a free ride!"

And flinging headships and abstractions to the winds, she raced the pair up to the chalet, where *Kaffee* was waiting on the veranda.

Late that night, as Gisela and Gottfried Mensch were strolling about their own garden before going to bed, Gisela turned to her husband with a question. "Gottfried, what do you think the school has done for Jo this term?"

He smiled down at her.

"So you remember what I said that night, little wife? Well, I think it has deepened her, and strengthened her. She will make a noble woman some day – one that the school may well be proud to number among its former pupils. She has great gifts – her ability to write – her voice – but, best of all, her great charm, which will always give her much influence over others."

"And it will be always for good," added Gisela softly. "And for that the world will owe much to Madame and the Chalet School."

Founded 1989

Have you enjoyed this Chalet School book?

If so, you will be pleased to know that there are many others like you. The Friends of the Chalet School is an international fans' society founded in 1989 to foster friendship between Chalet School fans all over the world.

Join Friends of the Chalet School for
Quarterly Newsletters over 60 pages long
A Lending Library of Rare Titles
Le Petit Chalet (for those aged 13 and under)
Sales and Wants
and
Chalet Merchandise

For more information send an A5 SAE to Ann Mackie-Hunter or Clarissa Cridland, 4 Rock Terrace, Coleford, Bath BA3 5NF, UK.

If you live outside the UK, please send an international reply coupon to the above address. We especially welcome members from outside the UK and there are FOCS local subscription co-ordinators in several countries to offset the cost of sending membership fees to the UK.

The New Chalet Club

Grüß Gott!
Calling Chalet School fans
of all ages.

Have you joined THE NEW CHALET
CLUB yet?
We produce quarterly journals with a special
junior section.
We have competitions and social events.
There are New Chalet Club members
world wide.

Write with SAE or IRC to

Helen Aveling (Membership Secretary)
1 Carpenter Court,
Neath Hill,
Milton Keynes,
Bucks, MK14 6JP,
UK.

We look forward to hearing from you.

Order Form

To order direct from the publishers, just make a list of the titles you want and fill in the form below:

Name

....

Address

....

....

....

Send to: Dept 6, HarperCollins Publishers Ltd, Westerhill Road, Bishopbriggs, Glasgow G64 2QT.

Please enclose a cheque or postal order to the value of the cover price, plus:

UK & BFPO: Add £1.00 for the first book, and 25p per copy for each additional book ordered.

Overseas and Eire: Add £2.95 service charge. Books will be sent by surface mail but quotes for airmail despatch will be given on request.

A 24-hour telephone ordering service is available to holders of Visa, MasterCard, Amex or Switch cards on 0141- 772 2281.

Collins
An *Imprint* of HarperCollins*Publishers*